Primo Levi was born in Turin in 1919, and graduated with honours in chemistry shortly before the racial laws prohibited Jews from taking academic degrees. In 1943 he joined a partisan group in northern Italy and was arrested and transported to Auschwitz. It was his knowledge as a chemist which saved his life. His camp was liberated in 1945, and Primo Levi was then sent with other Italians to White Russia. After his return to Italy, he continued to work as a chemist until his retirement in 1975. Primo Levi died in April 1987.

Apart from *The Drowned and the Saved* (*I Sommersi e i salvati*; 1986), Primo Levi's other works are *If This Is a Man* (*Se questo è un uomo*; 1958), *The Truce* (*La Tregua*; 1963, winner of the Premio Campiello), *Natural Stories* (*Storie Naturali*; 1967, winner of the Premio Bagutta), *A Structural Defect* (*Vizio di Forma*; 1971), *The Wrench* (*La Chiave a Stella*; 1979, winner of the Premio Strega), *The Periodic Table* (*Il Sistema Periodico*; 1975, winner of the Premio Prato), *Moments of Reprieve* (*Lilit e altri racconti*; 1981) and *If Not Now, When?* (*Se Non Ora, Quando?*; 1982, winner of the Premio Campiello and the Viareggio prize). In addition, he wrote a volume of poetry, *Shema*.

# THE DROWNED
# AND
# THE SAVED

## Primo Levi

*Translated by*
*Raymond Rosenthal*

*Introduction by*
*Paul Bailey*

SPHERE BOOKS LTD

Published by the Penguin Group
27 Wrights Lane, London W8 5TZ, England
Viking Penguin Inc., 40 West 23rd Street, New York, New York 10010, USA
Penguin Books Australia Ltd, Ringwood, Victoria, Australia
Penguin Books Canada Ltd, 2801 John Street, Markham, Ontario, Canada L3R 1B4
Penguin Books (NZ) Ltd, 182–190 Wairau Road, Auckland 10, New Zealand

Penguin Books Ltd, Registered Offices: Harmondsworth, Middlesex, England

First published in Great Britain by Michael Joseph Ltd 1988
Published by Sphere Books Ltd 1989
Originally published in Italian under the title *I Sommersi e i salvati*

Copyright © 1986 by Giulio Einaudi editore s.p.a.
This translation copyright © 1988 by Simon & Schuster, Inc.
Introduction copyright © 1988 by Paul Bailey
All rights reserved

Printed and bound in Great Britain by
Richard Clay Ltd, Bungay, Suffolk

Since then, at an uncertain hour,
That agony returns,
And till my ghastly tale is told
This heart within me burns.

Samuel Taylor Coleridge.
*The Rime of the Ancient Mariner*
ll 582–85

# Contents

# Contents

# Introduction

## PAUL BAILEY

'We, the survivors, are not the true witnesses' – that deeply held conviction informs virtually everything Primo Levi wrote. The 'true witnesses' – those, that is, in full possession of the terrible truth – are the *sommersi*: the drowned, the submerged, the annihilated. They were not merely destroyed, they were blotted out of existence:

> The human ashes coming from the crematoria, tons daily, were easily recognised as such, because they often contained teeth or vertebrae. Nevertheless, they were employed for several purposes: as fill for swamp lands, as thermal insulation between the walls of wooden buildings, and as phosphate fertiliser; and, especially notable, they were used instead of gravel to cover the paths of the SS village near the camp. I couldn't say whether out of pure callousness or because, due to its origins, it was regarded as material to be trampled on.

'We speak in their stead, by proxy,' Levi says of himself and those others among the *salvati*, the saved, who have written of their experience of the concentration camps. In this, his last book, he speaks with a sometimes fierce eloquence for the millions of witnesses who disappeared. It is a book in which the questions outnumber the answers, for all Levi's brave attempts to explain the inexplicable. The verb *decifrare*, to decipher, occurs frequently in the text. The appalling code that is Nazism, he acknowledges, has only been partially cracked. *The Drowned and the Saved* dispels the myth that Primo

Levi forgave the Germans for what they did to his people. He didn't, and couldn't, forgive. He refused, however, to indulge in what he called 'the bestial vice of hatred', which is an entirely different matter. The voice that sounds in his writing is that of a reasonable man, dismayed by the lack of reasonableness in his fellow human beings. It's the voice of a sceptic, a natural doubter. In the eighth chapter, 'Letters from Germans', he tells of a friendship that developed between himself and Hety S. of Wiesbaden. After the publication of Levi's first book, *If This is a Man*, in Germany, Hety S. wrote to him to say that the memoir had 'awakened some resonance' in her country. In his reply, Levi noted that it had indeed 'awakened some resonance', 'but actually among the Germans who least needed to read it: I had received penitent letters from the innocent, not the guilty. These, understandably, were silent.'

The German edition of *If This is a Man* is prefaced by a letter Levi wrote to his translator. In it he remarks that writing about his time in Auschwitz had given him not only maturity but a reason for living. (Readers of *The Periodic Table* will recall that Levi lived a zombie-like existence in the months immediately following his liberation, before he made the momentous decision to confront his fearsome memories with the aid of words.) The letter goes on:

Perhaps it is presumption: but there it is, today I, prisoner No. 174517, by your help, can speak to the German people, remind them of what they have done, and say to them: 'I am alive, and I would like to understand you in order to judge you.'

It continues:

I never harboured hatred for the German people. And if I had felt that way, I would be cured of it after having known you. I do not understand, I cannot tolerate the fact that a man should be judged not for what he is but because of the group to which he happens to belong . . .

And this is how it ends:

> But I cannot say I understand the Germans: now, some-
> thing one cannot understand constitutes a painful void, a
> puncture, a permanent stimulus that insists on being satis-
> fied. I hope that this book will have some echo in Ger-
> many, not only out of ambition, but also because the
> nature of this echo will perhaps make it possible for me
> to better understand the Germans, placate this stimulus.

*If This is a Man* has definitely had some echo in Germany,
where it has been reprinted several times. Among the earliest
Germans to respond to Levi's 'painful void' was a certain Dr
T. H. of Hamburg, who cannot be described as innocent. In
the course of a meandering, near-defence of the Third Reich,
the doctor assures Levi that, in 1933, Hitler was the lesser of
two evils. National Socialism had to be preferred to Com-
munism. 'That all his beautiful words were falsehood and
betrayal we did not understand at the beginning.' Later in this
calculated exercise in hand-wringing, he dares to observe that
Hitler's 'insensate hatred for the Jews' was 'never popular'. He
adds: 'Germany deservedly counted as the country most
friendly to the Jews in the entire world.'

Dr T.H.'s letter – from which Levi quotes with a barely
controlled disgust – concludes on a sickeningly 'personal' note:

> Dear Dr Levi (I take the liberty to address you like this,
> because anyone who has read your book cannot but hold
> you dear), I have no excuses. I have no explanations. The
> guilt weighs heavily on my poor betrayed and misguided
> people. Rejoice for the life that has been given to you
> again, the peace of your beautiful country that I too
> know. Also Dante and Boccaccio have their place on my
> shelf. Your most devoted, T. H.

The normally temperate Primo Levi 'answered with a long
letter, perhaps the only irate one I ever wrote'. Levi corrected

the doctor's distorted version of recent German history, and put him right on Christian teaching. He also informed the Italophile, with characteristic irony, that he kept Hitler's *Mein Kampf* on *his* shelf, next to Dante and Boccaccio. 'Nothing is lacking in that book: the blood and the land, the living space, the Jew as the eternal enemy, the Germans who embody "the highest form of humanity on earth", the other countries openly regarded as the instruments of German domination.' These, Levi reminded the false penitent, are not 'beautiful words' – 'perhaps Hitler also uttered other words, but he never retracted these'.

There were no 'beautiful words' in the Lagers. 'It is an obvious observation that where violence is inflicted on man, it is also inflicted on language,' Levi writes in the fourth chapter, entitled 'Communicating'. Each Lager had its own peculiar jargon, a mixture of old Prussian terms and words newly invented by the SS. This was not the German of Heine and Goethe – 'melodious, refined' – but a sub-language, 'a language apart'; it was *Orts-und zeitgebunden*, 'tied to the place and time'. In the sixth chapter, 'The Intellectual in Auschwitz', Primo Levi considers the linguistic hell into which the Austrian philosopher Hans Mayer, who re-named himself Jean Améry, was plunged. The barbaric jargon caused him spiritual anguish. 'He suffered from it *because* German was his language, because he was a philologist who loved his language: just as a sculptor would suffer at seeing one of his statues befouled or muti-lated.' ... *che gli scorticava la bocca se cercava di parlarlo*: 'it scorched his mouth when he tried to speak it'.

Améry killed himself in 1978. Before he was deported to Auschwitz, Améry had been tortured by the Gestapo because of his work in the Belgian resistance. 'Anyone who has been tortured remains tortured,' Améry wrote. 'Anyone who has suffered torture never again will be able to be at ease in the world ... Faith in humanity, already cracked by the first slap in the face, is never acquired again.' For Améry, Levi remarks, torture was 'an interminable death'.

There can be no doubt that Améry's suicide affected Primo

Levi profoundly. The argument Levi conducts with his ghost in *The Drowned and the Saved* is especially poignant in the light of Levi's own self-inflicted death. It's a persuasive argument, the more so for being based on dreadful personal experience. Améry, who had severely constricted ideas about what constitutes an intellectual, maintained that intellectuals suffered more in the Lagers than their less gifted fellow prisoners. Levi takes issue with this simplification, with his customary disrespect for the half-truth and the easy answer. Levi claims that he wasn't a fully-fledged intellectual during his internment, but he was curious about what was going on around him, and that curiosity was one of the contributory factors to his surviving. The Lager was his university, in a sense. Unlike Améry, he learned from the artisans in the camp that physical labour, dutifully undertaken, brings fulfilment. He came to understand the dignity a carpenter or a builder feels when he has successfully completed a difficult task. He faced the challenge of what he calls *un 'misurarsi' conradiano*, 'a Conradian "testing of oneself"'. 'The Intellectual in Auschwitz' ends with this resonant sentence: 'The aims of life are the best defence against death: and not only in the Lager.'

The sentence is crucial to an understanding of Levi's achievement as a man and as a writer. Since his suicide on 11 April 1987, there has been a great amount of speculation: the third chapter of *The Drowned and the Saved*, which deals with the shame suffered by the survivors of the camps – shame at being alive, when so many are so horribly dead – has even been cited as 'evidence' that Levi intended to kill himself one day. Actually, it isn't at all evident from the chapter that Levi had any such thing in mind. It's true that he speaks of a shame that is 'concrete, heavy, perennial' and he mourns the absence in the world of brave and decent men like Chaim, the watchmaker from Cracow, who taught Levi the essential rules for survival, despite the language barrier; like the Hungarian, Szabo, who helped his weaker companions to do their daily quota of manual work; and like Baruch, a docker from Livorno, who returned the obligatory punches that were

heaped on him in good measure. He was immediately massacred, by no less than three *Kapos*, for his 'insolence'. 'These,
and innumerable others, died not in spite of their valour but
because of it.'

Levi was aware that his sense of shame had little justification
in reality, for he had not been responsible for the death of a
single human being. Yet he couldn't prevent himself from
thinking that the best had perished in the gas chambers, and
that the worst had survived. It is undeniable, however, that
Levi used that shame both positively and creatively: it spurred
him on, it led him to ask question after pertinent question. He
may not have come to terms with it, but he had found a way
in which it could be made applicable to the aims of his life.

Améry's suicide, Levi observes, 'like other suicides, allows
for a nebula of explanations'. The same has to be said of his
own. Had Levi planned his death, which is doubtful, he would
surely have carried out his plan in the most efficacious manner,
with the aid of drugs, perhaps. He was, after all, a chemist by
profession. His suicide, though, was sudden and violent. He
hurled himself down the stairwell in the apartment building in
Turin where he had been born and where he had spent the
greater part of his life. According to two of his closest friends,
Livio Norzi and Bianca Guidetti Serra, Levi had been weighed
down with entirely personal problems in the days before his
death: he had undergone an operation for cancer of the pros-
tate, and he was depressed by the condition of his beloved
mother, who was enduring all the indignities attendant on
extreme age. It is their conviction that Levi, who had been
prescribed anti-depressant drugs by his doctor, must have had
some kind of brainstorm.

To speculate further is as pointless as it is distasteful. What
is abundantly clear is that Primo Levi, in everything he wrote –
including this, his darkest work – was on the side of life. *The
Drowned and the Saved* warns and reminds us that the un-
imaginable can happen again. A would-be tyrant is waiting in
the wings, with 'beautiful words' on his lips. The book is
constantly impressing on us the need to learn from the past, to

make sense of the senseless. As he grew older, Levi came to see himself as an ancient mariner of sorts, fixing people with his glittering eye and insisting that they listen. Hence the epigraph, with its apt verse from Coleridge's masterpiece.

As always, Levi assumes the role of the witness in *The Drowned and the Saved*. He amasses the evidence, and leaves the judgement to his readers. His comments on those unhappy prisoners who were forced, for a multitude of different reasons, to collaborate with their captors to a greater or lesser extent, are notable for the wary compassion with which they are expressed. The chapter in which they appear, 'The Grey Zone', is the most harrowing in the book, with its chilling recollections of the activities of the *corvi del crematorio*, 'the crematorium crows'.

No one, Levi argues, is in a position to judge these unfortunates, most of whom were obliterated in due course because of their knowledge of the workings of the gas chambers. The truth died with them. 'It has been testified that a large amount of alcohol was put at the disposal of those wretches and that they were in a permanent state of complete debasement and prostration. One of them declared: "Doing this work, one either goes crazy the first day or gets accustomed to it." Another, though: "Certainly, I would have killed myself or got myself killed; but I wanted to survive, to avenge myself and bear witness. You mustn't think we are monsters; we are the same as you, only much more unhappy."'

In that same chapter, Levi quotes some fashionable drivel evacuated by the film director, Liliana Cavani, she of *The Night Porter*. 'We are all victims of murderers, and we accept these roles voluntarily. Only Sade and Dostoevsky have really understood this . . . In every environment, in every relationship, there is a victim–executioner dynamism more or less clearly expressed and generally lived on an unconscious level.' Levi's reaction to these pronouncements is typically caustic:

I am not an expert of the unconscious and the mind's depths, but I do know that few people are the experts in this sphere, and that these few are the most cautious; I do not know, and it does not much interest me to know, whether in my depths there lurks a murderer, but I do know that I was a guiltless victim and I was not a murderer; I know that the murderers existed, not only in Germany, and still exist, retired or on active duty, and that to confuse them with their victims is a moral disease or an aesthetic affection or a sinister sign of complicity; above all, it is a precious service rendered (intentionally or not) to the negators of truth.

'The negators of truth': they are mankind's constant enemy, Levi insists. Towards the close of *The Drowned and the Saved*, he offers us a salutary reminder of the importance of truthfulness, of individual honesty:

I must nevertheless admit that I experienced (and again only once) the temptation to yield, to seek refuge in prayer. This happened in the October of 1944, in the one moment in which I lucidly perceived the imminence of death: when, naked and compressed among my naked companions with my personal index card in hand, I was waiting to file past the 'commission' that with one glance would decide whether I should immediately go into the gas chamber or was instead strong enough to go on working. For one instant I felt the need for help and asylum; then, despite my anguish, equanimity prevailed: one does not change the rules of the game at the end of the match, nor when you are losing. A prayer under these conditions would have been not only absurd (what rights could I claim? and from whom?) but blasphemous, obscene, laden with the greatest impiety of which a non-believer is capable. I rejected that temptation: I know that otherwise were I to survive, I would have to be ashamed of it.

Primo Levi seems to me to be one of that select band of

writers with whom it is possible to sustain a lasting friendship. One can turn to him for advice and help. He has a hard-won wisdom, and that wisdom will ensure his survival. He kept faith, in his faithlessness. His books offer us what Geoffrey Grigson detected in the best poetry of W. H. Auden: 'Explicit recipes for being human.'

*Paul Bailey, London 1987*

# THE DROWNED
# AND THE SAVED

# Preface

The first news about the Nazi annihilation camps began to spread in the crucial year, 1942. They were vague pieces of information, yet in agreement with each other: they delineated a massacre of such vast proportions, of such extreme cruelty and such intricate motivation that the public was inclined to reject them because of their very enormity. It is significant that this rejection was foreseen well in advance by the culprits themselves; many survivors (among others, Simon Wiesenthal in the last pages of *The Murderers Are Among Us*) remember that the SS militiamen cynically enjoyed admonishing the prisoners:

'However this war may end, we have won the war against you; none of you will be left to bear witness, but even if someone were to survive, the world would not believe him. There will perhaps be suspicions, discussions, research by historians, but there will be no certainties, because we will destroy the evidence together with you. And even if some proof should remain and some of you survive, people will say that the events you describe are too monstrous to be believed: they will say that they are the exaggerations of Allied propaganda and will believe us, who will deny everything, and not you. We will be the ones to dictate the history of the Lagers.'

Strangely enough, this same thought ('even if we were to tell it, we would not be believed') arose in the form of nocturnal dreams produced by the prisoners' despair. Almost all the survivors, verbally or in their written memoirs, remember a

dream which frequently recurred during the nights of imprisonment, varied in its detail but uniform in its substance:
they had returned home and with passion and relief were describing their past sufferings, addressing themselves to a loved
person, and were not believed, indeed were not even listened
to. In the most typical (and most cruel) form, the interlocutor
turned and left in silence. This is a theme to which we shall
return, but at this point it is important to emphasise how both
parties, victims and oppressors, had a keen awareness of the
enormity and therefore the non-credibility of what took place
in the Lagers: and, we may add here, not only in the Lagers,
but in the ghettos, the rear areas of the Eastern front, the
police stations, and the asylums for the mentally handicapped.

Fortunately, things did not go as the victims feared and the
Nazis hoped. Even the most perfect of organisations has its
flaws, and Hitler's Germany, especially during the last months
before the collapse, was far from being a perfect machine.
Much material evidence of the mass exterminations was
suppressed, or a more or less dextrous attempt was made to
suppress them: in the autumn of 1944 the Nazis blew up the
gas chambers and crematoria in Auschwitz, but the ruins
remain, and despite the contortions of later generations it is
difficult to justify their function by having recourse to fanciful
hypotheses. The Warsaw ghetto, after the famous insurrection
in the spring of 1943, was razed to the ground, but thanks to
the superhuman concern of a number of fighter-historians (historians of themselves!) who made certain that in the rubble,
often many metres deep, or smuggled beyond the wall, testimony survived, other historians could rediscover how, day by
day, the ghetto lived and died. All the archives in the Lagers
were burned during the last days of the war, and that was
truly an irremediable loss, so that even today there is discussion
as to whether the victims were four, six, or eight million:
though one still talks of millions.

Before the Nazis had recourse to the gigantic multiple
crematoria, the innumerable corpses of the victims, deliberately
killed or worn down by hardships and illnesses, could consti-

tute evidence and must somehow be made to disappear. The first solution, macabre to the point of making one hesitate to speak of it, had been that of simply piling up the bodies, hundreds of thousands of bodies, in huge common graves, and this was done, in particular at Treblinka and other minor Lagers, and in the wake of the German army in Russia. This was a temporary solution decided upon with bestial insouciance when the German armies were winning on all fronts and final victory appeared certain; afterwards one would decide what should be done. In any case, the victor is the master even of truth and can manipulate it as he pleases: somehow, the common graves would be justified, or made to disappear, or attributed to the Soviets (who, for that matter, proved at Katyn not to be lagging too far behind). But after Stalingrad, there were second thoughts: best to erase everything immediately. The prisoners themselves were forced to exhume those pitiful remains and burn them on pyres in the open, as if an operation of such proportions and so unusual could go completely unnoticed.

The SS command posts and the security services then took the greatest care to ensure that no witness would survive. This is the meaning (it would be difficult to devise another) of the murderous and apparently insane transfers with which the history of the Nazi camps came to an end during the first months of 1945: the survivors of Maidanek to Auschwitz, those of Auschwitz to Buchenwald and Mauthausen, those of Buchenwald to Bergen-Belsen, the women of Ravensbrück in the direction of Schwerin. In short, everyone must be snatched away from liberation, deported again to the heart of Germany which was being invaded from the west and east; it did not matter that they might die along the way, what really mattered was that they should not tell their story. In fact, having functioned as centres of political terror, then as death factories, and subsequently (or simultaneously) as immense reservoirs of ever renewed slave labour, the Lagers had become dangerous for a moribund Germany because they contained the secret of the Lagers themselves, the greatest crime in the history of humanity. The army of ghosts that still vegetated in them was composed of *Geheinnisfräger*, the bearers of secrets who must be disposed of. The extermination plants, also very eloquent, having been destroyed, the decision was made to move them to the interior, in the absurd hope of still being able to lock them up in Lagers less threatened by the advancing fronts, and exploit their final ability to work, and in the other, less absurd hope, that the torment of those Biblical marches would reduce their number. In fact their number *was* appallingly reduced, yet some nevertheless had the luck or the strength to survive and remained to bear witness.

Less well known and less studied is the fact that many bearers of secrets were also on the other side, though many knew little and few knew everything. No one will ever be able to establish with precision how many, in the Nazi apparatus, could *not not know* about the frightful atrocities that were being committed; how many knew something but were in a position to pretend that they did not know; and, further, how many had the possibility of knowing everything, but chose the more prudent path of keeping their eyes and ears (and above all their mouths) well shut. Whatever the case, since one cannot suppose that the majority of Germans lightheartedly accepted the slaughter, it is certain that the failure to divulge the truth about the Lagers represents one of the major collective crimes of the German people, and the most obvious demonstration of the cowardice to which Hitlerian terror had reduced them: a cowardice which became an integral part of mores, and so profound as to prevent husbands from telling their wives, parents their children. Without this cowardice the greatest excesses would not have been carried out, and Europe and the world would be different today.

Without a doubt those who knew the horrible truth because they were (or had been) responsible, had compelling reasons to be silent; but, inasmuch as they were depositories of the secret, even by keeping silent they could not always be sure of remaining alive. This is proved by the case of Stangl and the other Treblinka butchers, who after the insurrection there and the dismantling of that Lager, were transferred to one of the most dangerous Partisan areas.

Willed ignorance and fear also led many potential 'civilian' witnesses of the infamies of the Lagers to remain silent. Especially during the last years of the war, the Lagers constituted an extensive and complex system which profoundly penetrated the daily life of the country; one has with good reason spoken of the *univers concentrationnaire*, but it was not a closed universe. Small and large industrial companies, agricultural combines, agencies and arms factories drew profits from the practically free labour supplied by the camps. Some exploited the prisoners pitilessly, accepting the inhuman (and also stupid) principle of the SS, according to which one prisoner was worth another, and if the work killed him he could immediately be replaced; others, a few, cautiously tried to alleviate their sufferings. Still other industries – or perhaps the same ones – made money out of supplying the Lagers themselves: lumber, building materials, the cloth for the prisoners' striped uniforms, the dehydrated vegetables for the soup, etc. The crematoria ovens themselves were designed, built, assembled and tested by a German company, Topf of Wiesbaden. (It was still in operation in 1975, building crematoria for civilian use, and had not considered the advisability of changing its name.) It is hard to believe that the personnel of these companies did not realise the significance of the quality or quantity of the merchandise and installations that were commissioned by the SS command units. The same can be said, and has been said, with regard to the supplies of the poison employed in the gas chambers at Auschwitz: the product, substantially hydrocyanic acid, had already been used for many years for pest control in the holds of boats, but the abrupt increase in orders beginning with 1942 could scarcely go unnoticed. It must have aroused doubts, and certainly did arouse them, but they were stifled by fear, the desire for profit, the blindness and willed stupidity that we have mentioned, and in some cases (probably few) by fanatical Nazi obedience.

It is natural and obvious that the most substantial material for the reconstruction of truth about the camps is constituted by the memories of the survivors. Beyond the pity and indignation they arouse, they should also be read with a critical eye. For knowledge of the Lagers, the Lagers themselves were not always a good observation post. In the inhuman conditions to which they were subjected, the prisoners could barely acquire an overall vision of their universe. It could happen, above all for those who did not understand German, that the prisoners did not even know in what part of Europe the Lager in which they were was situated and to which they had arrived after a slaughterous and tortuous journey in sealed boxcars. They did not know about the existence of other Lagers, even those only a few kilometres away. They did not know for whom they worked. They did not understand the significance of certain sudden changes in conditions, and of the mass transfers. Surrounded by death, the deportee was often in no position to evaluate the extent of the slaughter that unfolded before his eyes. The companion who worked beside him today was no longer there on the morrow: he might be in the hut next door, or erased from the world; there was no way to know. In short, he felt overwhelmed by an enormous edifice of violence and menace but could not form for himself a representation of it because his eyes were fastened to the ground by every single minute's needs.

This deficiency conditioned the verbal or written testimonies of the 'normal' prisoners, those not privileged, the ones who represented the core of the camps and who escaped death only by a combination of improbable events. They were the majority in the Lager, but an exiguous minority among the survivors: among them, those who during their imprisonment enjoyed some sort of privilege are much more numerous. At a distance of years one can today definitely affirm that the history of the Lagers has been written almost exclusively by those who, like myself, never fathomed them to the bottom. Those who did so did not return, or their capacity for observation was paralysed by suffering and incomprehension.

On the other hand, the 'privileged' witnesses could avail

themselves certainly of a better observatory, if only because it was located higher up and hence took in a more extensive horizon; but it was to a greater or lesser degree also falsified by the privilege itself. The discussion concerning privilege (not only in the Lager) is delicate, and I shall try to go into it later with the greatest possible objectivity: here I will only mention the fact that the privileged *par excellence*, that is, those who acquired privilege for themselves by becoming subservient to the camp authority, did not bear witness at all, for obvious reasons, or left incomplete, distorted or totally false testimony. Therefore, the best historians of the Lagers emerged from among the very few who had the ability and luck to attain a privileged observatory without bowing to compromises, and the skill to tell what they saw, suffered and did with the humility of a good chronicler, taking into account the complexity of the Lager phenomenon and the variety of human destinies being played out in it.

It was in the logic of things that these historians should almost all be political prisoners: and this because the Lagers were a political phenomenon; because the political prisoners, much more than the Jews and the criminals (these, as is known, were the three principal categories of prisoners), disposed of a cultural background which allowed them to interpret the events which they saw; because, precisely inasmuch as they were ex-combatants or anti-Fascist combatants even now, they realised that testimony was an act of war against Fascism; because they had easier access to statistical data; and lastly, because often, besides holding important positions in the Lager, they were members of the secret defence organisation. At least during the last years, their living conditions were tolerable, which permitted them, for example, to write and preserve notes; a thing which for the Jews was unthinkable, and which the criminals were not interested in doing.

For all the reasons touched on here, the truth about the Lagers has come to light through a long road and a narrow door, and many aspects of the *univers concentrationnaire* still have not been explored in depth. By now, more than forty years have passed since the liberation of the Nazi Lagers; this considerable interval has, for the purposes of clarification, led to conflicting results, which I will try to enumerate.

In the first place, there has been the decanting, a desirable and normal process, thanks to which historical events acquire their chiaroscuro and perspective only some decades after their conclusion. At the end of the Second World War, quantitative data on the Nazi deportations and massacres, in the Lagers and elsewhere, had not been acquired, nor was it easy to understand their import and specificity. For only a few years now has one begun to understand that the Nazi slaughter was dreadfully 'exemplary' and that, if nothing worse happens in the coming years, it will be remembered as the central event, the scourge of this century.

By contrast, the passage of time has as its consequence other historically negative results. The greater part of witnesses, for the defence and the prosecution, have by now disappeared, and those who remain, and who (overcoming their remorse or, respectively, their wounds) still agree to testify, have ever more blurred and stylised memories; often, unbeknown to them, influenced by information they gained later from readings or the stories of others. In some cases, naturally, the lack of memory is simulated, but the many years that have gone by make it credible, also upon examination the 'I don't know' or 'I did not know' said today by many Germans no longer shocks us, but they did shock or should have shocked us when events were recent.

Of another or further stylisation we are ourselves responsible, we survivors, or, more precisely, those among us who have decided to live their condition as survivors in the most simple and least critical way. This does not mean that ceremonies and celebrations, monuments and flags are always and everywhere to be deplored. A certain dose of rhetoric is perhaps indispensable for the memory to persist. That sepulchres, 'the urns of the strong', kindle souls to perform lofty deeds, or at least preserve the memory of accomplished deeds, was true in Foscolo's time and is still true today; but one must beware of excessive simplifications. Every victim is to be mourned, and every survivor is to be helped and pitied, but not all their acts should be set forth as examples. The inside of the Lager was an intricate and stratified microcosm; the 'grey zone' of which I shall speak later, that of the prisoners who in some measure, perhaps with good intentions, collaborated with the authority, was not negligible, indeed it constituted a phenomenon of fundamental importance for the historian, the psychologist and the sociologist. There is not a prisoner who does not remember this, and who does not remember his amazement at the time: the first threats, the first insults, the first blows did not come from the SS but from other prisoners, from 'colleagues', from those mysterious personages who nevertheless wore the same striped tunic that they, the new arrivals, had just put on.

This book means to contribute to the clarification of some aspects of the Lager phenomenon which still appear obscure. It also sets for itself a more ambitious goal: it will try to answer the most urgent question, the question which torments all those who happened to read our accounts. How much of the concentration camp world is dead and will not return, like slavery and the duelling code? How much is back or is coming back? What can each of us do, so that in this world pregnant with threats, at least this threat will be nullified?

I did not intend to do, nor would I have been able to do, a historian's work; that is, exhaustively examine the sources. I have almost exclusively confined myself to the National Socialist Lagers because I had direct experience only of these: I also had a copious indirect experience of them, through books I read, stories I listened to, and encounters with the readers of my first two books. Besides, up to the moment at which I am writing, and notwithstanding the horror of Hiroshima and Nagasaki, the shame of the Gulags, the useless and bloody Vietnam war, the Cambodian self-genocide, the *desaparecidos* of Argentina, and the many atrocious and stupid wars we have seen since, the Nazi concentration camp system still remains a *unicum*, both in its extent and quality. In no other place and time has one seen a phenomenon so unexpected and so complex: never were so many human lives extinguished in so short a time, and with so lucid a combination of technological ingenuity, fanaticism and cruelty. No one wants to absolve the Spanish *conquistadores* of the massacres perpetrated in America throughout the sixteenth century. It seems they brought about the death of at least sixty million Indios; but they acted on their own, without or against the directives of their government; and they diluted their misdeeds – not very 'planned', to tell the truth – over a span of more than one hundred years; and they were also helped by the epidemics that they involuntarily brought with them. And, finally, did we not try to dispose of them by declaring that they were 'things of another time'?

# CHAPTER ONE

# The Memory of the Offence

Human memory is a marvellous but fallacious instrument. This is a threadbare truth known not only to psychologists but also to anyone who has paid attention to the behaviour of those who surround him, or even to his own behaviour. The memories which lie within us are not carved in stone; not only do they tend to become erased as the years go by, but often they change, or even increase by incorporating extraneous features. Judges know this very well: it almost never happens that two eyewitnesses of the same event describe it in the same way and with the same words, even if the event is recent and neither of them has a personal interest in distorting it. This scant reliability of our memory will be satisfactorily explained only when we know in what language, in what alphabet they are written, on what material, and with what pen: to this day we are still far from this goal. Some mechanisms are known which falsify memory under particular conditions: traumas, not only cerebral ones; interference by other 'competitive' memories; abnormal conditions of consciousness; repressions; blockages. Nevertheless, even under normal conditions a slow degradation is at work, an obfuscation of outlines, a, so-to-speak, physiological oblivion, which few memories resist. It is probable that one may recognise here one of the great powers of nature, the same that degrades order into disorder, youth into old age, and extinguishes life in death. It is certain that practice (in this case, frequent re-evocation) keeps memories fresh and alive in the same manner in which a muscle that is often used remains efficient; but it is also true that a memory evoked too often, and expressed in the form of a story, tends to become fixed in a stereotype, in a form tested by experience, crystallised, perfected, adorned, which installs itself in the place of the raw memory and grows at its expense.

I intend to examine here the memories of extreme experiences, of injuries suffered or inflicted. In this case, all or almost all the factors that can obliterate or deform the mnemonic record are at work. The memory of a trauma suffered or inflicted is itself traumatic because recalling it is painful or at least disturbing: a person who was wounded tends to block out the memory so as not to renew the pain; the person who has inflicted the wound pushes the memory deep down, to be rid of it, to alleviate the feeling of guilt.

Here, as with other phenomena, we are dealing with a paradoxical analogy between victim and oppressor, and we are anxious to be clear: both are in the same trap, but it is the oppressor, and he alone, who has prepared it and activated it, and if he suffers from this, it is right that he should suffer; and it is iniquitous that the victim should suffer from it, as indeed he does suffer from it, even at a distance of decades. Once again it must be observed, mournfully, that the injury cannot be healed: it extends through time, and the Furies, in whose existence we are forced to believe, not only wrack the tormentor (if they do wrack him, assisted or not by human punishment), but they perpetuate the tormentor's work by denying peace to the tormented. It is not without horror that we read the words left us by Jean Améry, the Austrian philosopher tortured by the Gestapo because he was active in the Belgian resistance and then deported to Auschwitz because he was Jewish:

> Anyone who has been tortured remains tortured . . . Anyone who has suffered torture never again will be able to be at ease in the world, the abomination of the annihilation is never extinguished. Faith in humanity, already cracked by the first slap in the face, then demolished by torture, is never acquired again.

Torture was for him an interminable death: Améry, about

whom I will speak again in Chapter Six, killed himself in 1978.

We do not wish to abet confusions, small-change Freudianism, morbidities and indulgences. The oppressor remains what he is, and so does the victim. They are not interchangeable, the former is to be punished and execrated (but, if possible, understood), the latter is to be pitied and helped; but both, faced by the indecency of the act which has been irrevocably committed, need refuge and protection, and instinctively search for them. Not all, but most; and often for their entire lives.

By now we are in possession of numerous confessions, depositions and admissions on the part of the oppressors (I speak not only of the German National Socialists, but of all those who commit horrendous and multiple crimes in obedience to a discipline): some given in court, others during interviews, others still contained in books or memoirs. In my opinion, these are documents of extreme importance. In general, the descriptions of the things seen and the acts committed are of little interest: they amply coincide with what was told by the victims; very rarely are they contested, judgements have been handed down and they are by now part of history. Often they are regarded as well known. Much more important are the motivations and justifications: why did you do this? Were you aware that you were committing a crime?

The answers to these two questions, or to others which are analogous, are very similar to each other, independent of the personality of the interrogated person, whether he be an ambitious and intelligent professional like Speer or a gelid fanatic like Eichmann, a short-sighted functionary like Stangl in Treblinka and Höss in Auschwitz, or an obtuse brute like Boger and Kaduk, the inventors of torture. Expressed in different formulations and with greater or lesser arrogance, depending on the speaker's mental and cultural level, in the end they all say substantially the same things: I did it because I was ordered to; others (my superiors) have committed acts worse than mine; in view of the upbringing I received, and the en-

vironment in which I lived, I could not act differently; if I had
not done it, another would have done it even more harshly in
my place. For anyone who reads these justifications the first
reaction is revulsion: they lie, they cannot believe they will be
believed, they cannot not see the imbalance between their
excuses and the enormity of pain and death that they have
caused. They lie knowing that they are lying: they are in bad
faith.

Now, anyone who has sufficient experience of human affairs
knows that the distinction (the opposition, a linguist would
say) good faith/bad faith is optimistic and illuminist, and is all
the more so, and for much greater reason, when applied to
men such as those just mentioned. It presupposes a mental
clarity which few have, and which even these few immediately
lose when, for whatever reason, past or present reality arouses
anxiety or discomfort in them. Under such conditions there
are, it is true, those who lie consciously, coldly falsifying reality
itself, but more numerous are those who weigh anchor, move
off, momentarily or forever, from genuine memories, and
fabricate for themselves a convenient reality. The past is a
burden to them; they feel repugnance for the things done or
suffered, and tend to replace them with others. The substitution
may begin in full awareness, with an invented scenario,
mendacious, restored, but less painful than the real one; in
repeating its description to others but also to themselves, the
distinction between true and false progressively loses its contours, and man ends by fully believing the story he has told so
many times and still continues to tell, polishing and retouching
here and there the details which are least credible or in-
congruous or incompatible with the acquired picture of historically accepted events: initial bad faith has become good faith.
The silent transition from falsehood to self-deception is useful:
anyone who lies in good faith is better off, he recites his part
better, is more easily believed by the judge, the historian, the
reader, his wife and his children.

The further events fade into the past, the more the con-
struction of convenient truth grows and is perfected. I believe

that only by this mental mechanism is it possible to interpret, for instance, the statements made in 1978 to *L'Express* by Louis Darquier de Pellepoix, former commissioner in charge of Jewish affairs in the Vichy government around 1942, and as such personally responsible for the deportation of 70,000 Jews. Darquier denies everything: the photographs of piles of corpses are montages; the statistics of millions of dead were fabricated by the Jews, always greedy for publicity, commiseration and indemnities. There may perhaps have been deportations (he would have found it difficult to dispute them: his signature appears at the foot of too many letters giving orders for these very deportations, even of children), but he did not know where to and with what results; there were, it is true, gas chambers in Auschwitz, but only to kill lice, and anyway (note the coherence!) they were built for propaganda purposes after the end of the war. It is not my intention to justify this cowardly and foolish man, and it offends me to know that he lived for a long time undisturbed in Spain, but I think I can recognise in him the typical case of someone who, accustomed to lying publicly, ends by lying in private too, to himself, and building for himself a comforting truth which allows him to live in peace. To keep good and bad faith distinct costs a lot: it requires a decent sincerity or truthfulness with oneself, it demands a continuous intellectual and moral effort. How can such an effort be expected from men like Darquier?

Reading the statements made by Eichmann during the Jerusalem trial, and those of Rudolph Höss (the penultimate commander of Auschwitz, the inventor of the hydrocyanic acid chambers) in his autobiography, one can see in them a process of re-elaboration of the past, more subtle than the one mentioned just above. In substance, these two defended themselves in the classical manner of the Nazi militia or, better yet, of all militiamen: we have been educated in absolute obedience, hierarchy, nationalism; we have been imbued with slogans, intoxicated with ceremonies and manifestations; we have been taught that the only justice was that which was to the advantage of our people, and the only truth were the words of the Leader.

What do you want from us? How can you even think to expect from us, after the fact, a behaviour different from what ours has been and that of all those who were like us? We were the diligent executors, and for our diligence we were praised and promoted. The decisions were not ours, because the regime in which we grew up did not allow us autonomous decisions: others have decided for us, and it could only happen that way, because our ability to decide had been amputated. So we are not responsible and cannot be punished.

Even projected against the background of the Birkenau smoke stacks, this reasoning cannot be considered purely the fruit of impudence. The pressure that a modern totalitarian state can exercise over the individual is frightful. Its weapons are substantially three: direct propaganda or propaganda camouflaged as upbringing, instruction and popular culture; the barrier erected against pluralism of information; and terror. Nevertheless, it is not permissible to admit that this pressure is irresistible, especially in the brief twelve-year term of the Third Reich, and in the affirmations and exculpations of men responsible for such serious crimes as were Höss and Eichmann, the exaggeration, and to an even greater degree the manipulation of memory, is obvious. Both were born and raised long before the Reich became truly 'totalitarian', and their joining the Nazi party was a choice dictated more by opportunism than enthusiasm. The re-elaboration of their past was a later work, slow and (probably) not methodical. To ask oneself whether it was done in good or bad faith is naïve. They too, so strong in the face of others' suffering, when fate put them before judges, before the death they deserved, built a convenient past for themselves and ended by believing in it: especially Höss, who was not a subtle man. As he appears in his writings, he was in fact a person so little inclined to self-control and introspection that he does not realise he is confirming his coarse anti-Semitism by the very act in which he abjures and denies it, nor does he realise how slimy his self-portrait as a good functionary, father and husband, actually is.

As a comment on these reconstructions of the past (but not

only on these: it is an observation that holds for all memories) one must note that the distortion of fact is often limited by the objectivity of the facts themselves, around or about which there exists the testimonies of third parties, documents, 'corpus delicti', historically accepted contexts. It is generally difficult to deny having committed a given act, or that such an act was committed; it is on the contrary very easy to alter the motivations which led us to an act, and the passions within us which accompanied the act itself. This is an extremely fluid matter, subject to being distorted even under very weak pressures. To the questions 'Why did you do this?' or 'What were you thinking as you did it?', no reliable answers exist, because states of mind are by nature labile and even more labile is the memory of them.

An extreme case of the distortion of the memory of a committed guilty act is found in its suppression. Here, too, the borderline between good and bad faith can be vague. Behind the 'I don't know' and the 'I do not remember' that one hears in courtrooms there is sometimes the precise intent to lie, but at other times it is a fossilised lie, rigidified in a formula. The rememberer has decided not to remember, and has succeeded: by dint of denying its existence, he has expelled the harmful memory as one expels an excretion or a parasite. Lawyers for the defence know very well that the memory gap, or the putative truth, which they suggest to their clients, tends to become forgetfulness and actual truth. It is not necessary to trespass in the field of mental pathology to find human examples whose declarations perplex us: they are most certainly false, but we are unable to detect whether the subject does or does not know he is lying. Supposing, absurdly, that the liar should for one instant become truthful, he himself would not know how to answer the dilemma; in the act of lying he is an actor totally fused with his part, he is no longer distinguishable from it. A glaring example of this, during the days in which I am writing, is the behaviour in court of the Turk Ali Agca, the would-be assassin of Pope John-Paul II.

The best way to defend oneself against the invasion of burdensome memories is to impede their entry, to extend a *cordon sanitaire*. It is easier to deny entry to a memory than to free oneself from it after it has been recorded. This, in substance, was the purpose of many of the artifices thought up by the Nazi commanders in order to protect the consciences of those assigned to do the dirty work, and to ensure their services, disagreeable even for the most hardened cut-throats. The *Einsatzkommandos*, who behind the front lines in Russia machine-gunned civilians at the side of common graves which the victims themselves had been forced to dig, were given all the liquor they wanted so that the massacre would be blurred by drunkenness. The well-known euphemisms ('final solution', 'special treatment', the very term *Einsatzkommando* just cited, which literally meant 'prompt-employment unit') disguised a frightful reality, were not only used to deceive the victims and prevent defensive reactions on their part: they were also meant, within the limits of the possible, to prevent public opinion, and those sections of the army that were not directly involved, from finding out what was happening in all the territories occupied by the Third Reich.

At any rate, the entire history of the brief 'millennial Reich' can be reread as a war against memory, an Orwellian falsification of memory, falsification of reality, negation of reality. All of Hitler's biographies, while disagreeing on the interpretation to be given to the life of this man so difficult to classify, agree on the flight from reality which marked his last years, beginning especially with the first Russian winter. He had forbidden and denied his subjects any access to truth, contaminating their morality and their memory; but, to a degree which gradually increased and attained complete paranoia in the Bunker, he barred the path of truth to himself also. Like all gamblers, he erected around himself a stage set woven out of superstitious lies, which he ended by believing with the same fanatical faith that he demanded from every German. His collapse was not only a salvation for mankind but also a demonstration of the price to be paid when one dismembers the truth.

*

In the vaster field of the victim one also observes a drifting of memory, but here, evidently, fraud is not involved. Anyone who receives an injustice or an injury does not need to elaborate lies to exculpate himself of a guilt he does not have (even though, due to a paradoxical mechanism of which we shall speak, it can happen that he feels ashamed of it); but this does not exclude the fact that his memories may also be altered. It has been noticed, for instance, that many survivors of wars or other complex and traumatic experiences tend unconsciously to filter their memory: summoning them up among themselves, or telling them to third persons, they prefer to dwell on moments of respite, on grotesque, strange or relaxed intermezzos, and to skim over the most painful episodes which are not called up willingly from the reservoir of memory, and therefore with time tend to mist over, lose their contours. The behaviour of Count Ugolino is psychologically credible when he becomes reticent about telling Dante of his terrible death, and he is induced to do so not out of acquiescence but only out of a feeling of posthumous revenge against his eternal enemy. When we say, 'I will never forget that', referring to some event which has profoundly wounded us but has not left in us or around us a material trace or a permanent void, we are foolhardy: in 'civilian' life we also gladly forget the details of a serious illness from which we have recovered, or those of a successful surgical operation.

For the purpose of defence, reality can be distorted not only in memory but in the very act of its taking place. Throughout the year of my imprisonment in Auschwitz I had Alberto D. as a fraternal friend: he was a robust, courageous young man, more clearsighted than the average and therefore very critical of the many who fabricated for themselves, and reciprocally administered to each other, consolatory illusions: 'the war will be over in two weeks', 'there will be no more selections', 'the English have landed in Greece', 'the Polish partisans are about to liberate the camp', and so on, rumours heard nearly every day and punctually given the lie by reality.

Alberto had been deported together with his forty-five-year-old father. In the imminence of the great selection of October 1944, Alberto and I had commented on this event with fright, impotent rage, rebellion, resignation but without seeking refuge in comforting truths. The selection came. Alberto's 'old' father was chosen for the gas, and in the space of a few hours Alberto changed. He had heard rumours that seemed to him worthy of belief: the Russians were close by, the Germans would no longer dare persist in the slaughter, that was not a selection like the others, it was not for the gas chamber, but had been made to choose the weakened but salvageable prisoners, like his father in fact, who was very tired but not ill; indeed, he even knew where they would be sent, to Jaworzno, not far away, to a special camp for convalescents fit only for light labour.

Naturally his father was never seen again and Alberto himself vanished during the evacuation march from the camp in January 1945. Strangely, without knowing about Alberto's behaviour, his relatives who had remained hidden in Italy, escaping capture, also behaved in the same way, rejecting an unendurable truth, constructing a different one for themselves. As soon as I was repatriated, I considered it my duty to go immediately to Alberto's home town to tell his mother and his brother what I knew. I was welcomed with courteous affection, but as soon as I began my story the mother begged me to stop: she already knew everything, at least as far as Alberto was concerned, and there was no point in my repeating the usual horror stories to her. She *knew* that her son, he alone, had been able to slip away from the column without being shot at by the SS, he had hidden in the forest and was safe in Russian hands; he had not yet been able to send any word, but he would do so soon, she was certain of it; and now, would I please change the subject, and tell her how I myself had survived. A year later I was by chance passing through that same town, and I again visited the family. The truth was slightly changed: Alberto was in a Soviet clinic, he was fine, but he had lost his memory, he no longer even remembered his name; he was improving though and would soon return – she had this from a reliable source.

Alberto never returned. More than forty years have passed; I did not have the courage to show up again and to counterpose my painful truth to the consolatory 'truth' that, one helping the other, Alberto's relatives had fashioned for themselves.

An apology is in order. This very book is drenched in memory; what's more, a distant memory. Thus it draws from a suspect source, and must be protected against itself. So here then: it contains more considerations than memories, lingers more willingly on the state of affairs such as it is now than on the retroactive chronicle. Furthermore, the data it contains are strongly substantiated by the imposing literature that has been formed around the theme of the man submerged (or 'saved'), and through the collaboration, voluntary or not, of the culprits of that time; and in this corpus the concordances are abundant, the discordances negligible. As for my personal memories, and the few unpublished anecdotes I have mentioned and will mention, I have diligently examined all of them: time has somewhat faded them, but they are in good consonance with their background and seem to me unaffected by the drifting I have described.

# CHAPTER TWO

# The Grey Zone

Have we – we who have returned – been able to understand and make others understand our experience? What we commonly mean by 'understand' coincides with 'simplify': without profound simplification the world around us would be an infinite, undefined tangle that would defy our ability to orient ourselves and decide upon our actions. In short, we are compelled to reduce the knowable to a schema: with this purpose in view we have built for ourselves admirable tools in the course of evolution, tools which are specifically the property of the human species – language and conceptual thought.

We also tend to simplify history; but the pattern within which events are ordered is not always identifiable in a single unequivocal fashion, and it may therefore happen that different historians understand and construe history in ways that are incompatible with one another. Nevertheless, perhaps for reasons that go back to our origins as social animals, the need to divide the field into 'we' and 'they' is so strong that this pattern, this bi-partition – friend–enemy – prevails over all others. Popular history, and also the history taught in schools, is influenced by this Manichean tendency which shuns half-tints and complexities: it is prone to reduce the river of human occurrences to conflicts, and the conflicts to duels – we and they, Athenians and Spartans, Romans and Carthaginians. This is certainly the reason for the enormous popularity of spectator sports, such as soccer, baseball and boxing, in which the contenders are two teams or two individuals, clearly distinct and identifiable, and at the end of the match there will be vanquished and victors. If the result is a draw, the spectator feels defrauded and disappointed: at the more or less un-conscious level, he wanted winners and losers and he identified them respectively with the good guys and the bad guys, because the good must prevail, otherwise the world would be sub-verted.

This *desire* for simplification is justified, but the same does not always apply to simplification itself. It is a working hypo-thesis, useful so long as it is recognised as such and not mis-taken for reality; the greater part of historical and natural phenomena is not simple, or not simple with the simplicity that we would like. Now, the network of human relationships inside the Lagers was not simple: it could not be reduced to the two blocs of victims and persecutors. In anyone who today reads (or writes) the history of the Lager is evident the tendency, indeed the need, to separate evil from good, to be able to take sides, to repeat Christ's gesture on Judgement Day: here the righteous, over there the reprobates. The young above all demand clarity, a sharp cut; their experience of the world being meagre, they do not like ambiguity. In any case, their ex-pectation reproduces exactly that of the newcomers to the Lagers, whether young or not; all of them, with the exception of those who had already gone through an analogous ex-perience, expected to find a terrible but decipherable world, in conformity to that simple model which we atavistically carry within us – 'we' inside and the enemy outside, separated by a sharply defined geographic frontier.

Instead, the arrival in the Lager was indeed a shock because of the surprise it entailed. The world into which one was precipi-tated was terrible, yes, but also indecipherable: it did not conform to any model, the enemy was all around but also inside, the 'we' lost its limits, the contenders were not two, one could not discern a single frontier but rather many confused, perhaps innumerable frontiers, which stretched between each of us. One entered hoping at least for the soli-darity of one's companions in misfortune, but the hoped-for allies, except in special cases, were not there; there were instead a thousand sealed-off monads, and in between them a desperate hidden and continuous struggle. This brusque revelation, which became manifest from the very first hours of imprisonment, often in the instant form of a concentric aggression on the part of those in whom one hoped to find future allies, was so harsh as to cause the immediate collapse of one's capacity to resist. For many it was lethal, indirectly or even directly: it is difficult to defend oneself against a blow for which one is not prepared.

Various aspects can be identified in this aggression. It is necessary to remember that the concentrationary system even from its origins (which coincide with the rise to power of Nazism in Germany) had the primary purpose of shattering the adversaries' capacity to resist: for the camp management, the new arrival was an adversary by definition, whatever the label attached to him might be, and he must immediately be demolished to make sure that he did not become an example or a germ of organised resistance. On this point the SS had very clear ideas and it is from this viewpoint that the entire sinister ritual there must be interpreted – varying from Lager to Lager, but basically similar – which accompanied the arrival: kicks and punches right away, often in the face; an orgy of orders screamed with true or simulated rage; complete nakedness after being stripped; the shaving off of all one's hair; the fitting out in rags. It is difficult to say whether all these details were devised by some expert or methodically perfected on the basis of experience, but they certainly were willed and not casual: it was all staged and this was quite obvious.

Nevertheless, the entry ritual, and the moral collapse which it promoted, was abetted more or less consciously by the other components of the concentrationary world: the simple prisoners and the privileged ones. It rarely happened that a newcomer was received, I won't say as a friend but at least as a companion in misfortune. In the majority of cases, those with seniority (and seniority was acquired in three or four months; the change-over was swift!) showed irritation or even hostility. The 'newcomer' (*Zugang:* one should note that in German this is an abstract, administrative term; it means 'access', 'entry') was envied because he still seemed to have on him the smell of his home. It was an absurd envy, because in fact one suffered much more during the first days of imprisonment than later on when habituation on the one hand and experience on the other made it possible to build oneself a shelter. He was derided and subjected to cruel pranks, as happens in all communities with 'conscripts' and 'rookies', and in the initiation ceremonies of primitive peoples: and there is no doubt that life in the Lager involved a regression, leading back precisely to primitive behaviour.

It is probable that the hostility towards the *Zugang* was in substance motivated like all other forms of intolerance; that is, it consisted in an unconscious attempt to consolidate the 'we' at the expense of the 'they', to create, in short, that solidarity among the oppressed whose absence was the source of additional suffering, even though not perceived openly. Vying for prestige also came into play, which in our civilisation seems to be an irrepressible need: the despised crowd of seniors was prone to recognise in the new arrival a target on which to vent its humiliation, to find compensation at his expense, to build for itself and at his expense a figure of a lower rank on whom to discharge the burden of the offences received from above.

As for the privileged prisoners, the situation was more complex, and also more important: in my opinion, it is in fact fundamental. It is naïve, absurd, and historically false to believe that an infernal system such as National Socialism was, sanctifies its victims: on the contrary, it degrades them, it makes them similar to itself, and this all the more when they are available, blank, and lack a political or moral armature.

From many signs, it would seem the time has come to explore the space which separates (and not only in Nazi Lagers) the victims from the persecutors, and to do so with a lighter hand, and with a less turbid spirit than has been done, for instance, in a number of films. Only a schematic rhetoric can claim that that space is empty: it never is; it is studded with obscene or pathetic figures (sometimes they possess both qualities simultaneously), whom it is indispensable to know if we

want to know the human species, if we want to know how to
defend our souls when a similar test should once more loom
before us, or even if we only want to understand what takes
place in a big industrial factory.

The privileged prisoners were a minority within the Lager
population, but they represent a potent majority among survivors; in fact, even if one does not take into account the hard
labour, the beatings, the cold, the illnesses, it must be remembered that the food ration was decisively insufficient even
for the most frugal prisoner: the physiological reserves of the
organism being consumed in two or three months, death by
hunger, or by diseases induced by hunger, was the prisoner's
normal destiny. This could be avoided only with additional
food, and to obtain it a large or small privilege was necessary;
in other words, a way, granted or conquered, astute or violent,
licit or illicit, to lift oneself above the norm.

Now, one mustn't forget that the greater part of the
memories of those who came back, told or written, begin in
this way: the collision with the concentrationary reality coincides with the unforeseen and uncomprehended aggression on
the part of a new and strange enemy, the functionary-prisoner,
who instead of taking you by the hand, reassuring you,
teaching you the way, throws himself at you, screaming in a
language you do not understand, and strikes you in the face.
He wants to tame you, extinguish in you the spark of dignity
that you perhaps still preserve and he has lost. But trouble is in
store for you if this dignity drives you to react: this is an un-
written but iron law. *Zurüchschlagen*, answering blows with
blows, is an intolerable transgression that can only occur to
the mind of a 'newcomer'. Anyone who commits it must be
made an example of: other functionaries rush to the defence of
the threatened order and the culprit is beaten with rage and
method until he's tamed or dead. Privilege, by definition, de-
fends and protects privilege. I remember now that the local,
Yiddish and Polish term to indicate privilege was '*protekcja*',
which is pronounced 'protekzia' and is of obvious Italian and
Latin origin. I was told the story of an Italian 'newcomer', a

Partisan, flung into a work Lager with the label of political prisoner when his strength was still at its height. He had been beaten when the soup was being distributed and had dared to shove the distributor-functionary: the latter's colleagues rushed to his help, and the culprit was made an example of by being drowned, his head held down in the soup tub.

The ascent of the privileged, not only in the Lager but in all human coexistence, is an anguishing but unfailing phenomenon: only in utopias are they absent. It is the duty of righteous men to make war on all undeserved privilege, but one must not forget that this is a war without end. Where there exists power exercised by the few or by only one against the many, privilege is born and proliferates, even against the will of the power itself; but on the other hand it is normal for power to tolerate and encourage it. Let us confine ourselves to the Lager which (even in its Soviet version) can be considered an excellent 'laboratory': the hybrid class of the prisoner-functionary constitutes its armature and at the same time its most disquieting feature. It is a grey zone, with ill-defined outlines which both separate and join the two camps of masters and servants. It possesses an incredibly complicated internal structure, and contains within itself enough to confuse our need to judge.

The grey zone of '*protekcja*' and collaboration is born from multiple roots. In the first place, the more the area of power is restricted, the more it needs external auxiliaries; the Nazism of the final years could not do without them, determined as it was to maintain its order within subjugated Europe and feed the front lines of the war bled white by its opponents' growing military resistance. It was indispensable to draw from the occupied countries not only labour but also forces of order, delegates and administrators of the German power which was by now committed elsewhere to the point of exhaustion. Within this area must be catalogued, with different nuances of quality and weight, Quisling in Norway, the Vichy government in France, the Judenrat in Warsaw, the Saló Republic in Italy, right down to the Ukrainian and Baltic mercenaries employed elsewhere for the filthiest tasks (never in combat) and the *Sonderkommandos*, about which we will have more to say.

But collaborators who originate in the adversary camp, ex-enemies, are untrustworthy by definition: they betrayed once and they can betray again. It is not enough to relegate them to marginal tasks; the best way to bind them is to burden them with guilt, cover them with blood, compromise them as much as possible. They will thus have established with their instigators the bond of complicity and will no longer be able to turn back. This way of proceeding is well known to criminal associations of all times and places, has always been practised by the Mafia and is also the only thing that can explain the otherwise indecipherable excesses of Italian terrorism in the 1970s.

In the second place, and in contrast with a certain hagiographic and rhetorical stylisation, the harsher the oppression, the more widespread among the oppressed is the willingness to collaborate with the power. This availability is also variegated by infinite nuances and motivations: terror, ideological seduction, servile imitation of the victor, myopic desire for any power whatsoever, even though ridiculously circumscribed in space and time, cowardice, and finally lucid calculation aimed at eluding the imposed orders and order. All these motives, singly or combined with one another, have been at work in originating this grey zone, whose components were held together by the wish to preserve and consolidate their privilege *vis-à-vis* those without privilege.

Before discussing separately the motives that impelled some prisoners to collaborate to a varying extent with the Lager authorities, it is necessary however to declare that before such human cases it is imprudent to hasten to issue a moral judgement. It must be clear that the greatest responsibility lies with the system, the very structure of the totalitarian state, the concurrent guilt on the part of the individual big and small collaborators (never likeable, never transparent!) is always difficult to evaluate. It is a judgement that we would like to entrust only to those who found themselves in similar circumstances, and had the possibility to test on themselves what it means to act in a state of coercion. Manzoni knew this quite well: 'Provocateurs, oppressors, all those who in some way injure others, are guilty, not only of the evil they commit, but also of the perversion into which they lead the spirit of the offended.' The condition of the offended does not exclude culpability, and this is often objectively serious, but I know of no human tribunal to which one could delegate the judgement.

If it were up to me, if I were forced to judge, I would light-heartedly absolve all those whose concurrence in the guilt was minimal and for whom coercion was of the highest degree. Around us, prisoners without rank, swarmed low-ranking functionaries. They formed a picturesque fauna: sweepers, kettle washers, night-watchmen, bed smoothers (who exploited to their minuscule advantage the German fixation about bunks made up flat and square), checkers of lice and scabies, messengers, interpreters, assistants' assistants. In general, they were poor devils like ourselves, who worked full time like everyone else, but who, for an extra half-litre of soup, were willing to carry out these and other 'tertiary' functions: innocuous, sometimes useful, often invented out of nothing. They were rarely violent, but they tended to develop a typically corporative mentality, and energetically defended their 'job' against anyone from below or above who might covet it. Their privilege, which at any rate entailed supplementary hardships and efforts, gained them very little and did not spare them from the discipline and suffering of everyone else; their hope for life was substantially the same as that of the unprivileged. They were coarse and arrogant, but they were not regarded as enemies.

Judgement becomes more delicate and varied for those who occupied commanding positions: the chiefs (*Kapos:* the German term derives directly from the Italian *capo*, and the truncated pronunciation, introduced by the French prisoners, spread only many years later, popularised by Pontecorvo's movie of the same name and preferred in Italy precisely because of its differentiating value) of the labour squads, the barracks chiefs, the clerks, all the way to the world (whose existence at that time I did not even suspect) of the prisoners who performed diverse, at times most delicate duties in the camps' administrative offices, the Political Section (actually a section of the Gestapo), the Labour Service, and the punishment cells. Some of these, thanks to skill or luck, had access to the most secret information of the respective Lagers and, like Herman Langbein in Auschwitz, Eugen Kogan in Buchenwald, and Hans Marsalek in Mauthausen, later became their historians. One does not know whether to admire more their personal courage or the cunning which enabled them concretely to help their companions in many ways, by attentively studying the individual SS officers with whom they had contact, and sensing who among them might be corrupted, who dissuaded from the crueller decisions, who blackmailed, who deceived, who frightened by the prospect of a *redde rationem* at the war's end. Some of them, the three mentioned above, for example, were also members of secret defence organisations, and therefore the power they wielded thanks to their positions was counterbalanced by the extreme danger they ran, inasmuch as they were both 'resistors' and the depositories of secrets.

The functionaries described were not at all, or only apparently, collaborators, but on the contrary were camouflaged opponents. Not so the greater part of the other persons with positions of command, who prove to be human specimens that range from the mediocre to the execrable. Rather than wearing one down, power corrupts; all the more intensely did their power corrupt, since it had a peculiar nature.

Power exists in all the varieties of the human social organisation, more or less controlled, usurped, conferred from above or recognised from below, assigned by merit, corporate solidarity, blood, or position: it is likely that a certain degree of man's domination over man is inscribed in our genetic patrimony as gregarious animals. It is not proved that power is intrinsically harmful to the collectivity. But the power of which the functionaries of whom we are speaking disposed, even if they were low-ranking, such as the *Kapos* of the work squads, was, in substance, unlimited; or, more accurately put, a lower limit was imposed on their violence, in the sense that they were punished or deposed if they did not prove to be sufficiently harsh, but there was no upper limit. In other words, they were free to commit the worst atrocities on their subjects as punishment for any transgressions, or even without any motive whatsoever. Until the end of 1943 it was not unusual for a prisoner to be beaten to death by a *Kapo*, without the latter having to fear any sanctions. Only later on, when the need for labour became more acute, a number of limitations were introduced: the mistreatment the *Kapos* were allowed to inflict on the prisoners must not permanently reduce their working ability; but by now the malpractice was established and the regulation was not always respected.

Thus inside the Lager, on a smaller scale but with amplified characteristics, was reproduced the hierarchical structure of the totalitarian state, in which all power is invested from above and control from below is almost impossible. But this 'almost' is important: there never existed a state that was really 'totalitarian' from this point of view. Some form of reaction, a corrective of the total tyranny has never been lacking, not even in the Third Reich or Stalin's Soviet Union: in both cases, public opinion, the magistrature, the foreign press, the churches, the feeling for justice and humanity which ten or twenty years of tyranny were not enough to eradicate, have to a greater or lesser extent acted as a brake. Only in the Lager was the restraint from below non-existent, and the power of these small satraps was absolute. It is understandable that power of such magnitude overwhelmingly attracted the human type who is greedy for power: that even individuals with moderate instincts aspired to it, seduced by the many material advantages of the position, and that the latter became fatally intoxicated by the power at their disposal.

Who became a *Kapo*? It is once again necessary to distinguish. In the first place, those to whom this possibility was offered, that is, those individuals in whom the Lager commander or his delegates (who were often good psychologists) discerned a potential collaborator: common criminals, taken from prisons, to whom a career as torturers offered an excellent alternative to detention; political prisoners broken by five or ten years of sufferings, or, in any case, morally debilitated; later on, also Jews who saw in the particle of authority that was being offered them the only possibility of escaping the 'final solution'. But many, as we mentioned, spontaneously aspired to power. It was sought by sadists, certainly not numerous but very much feared, because for them the position of privilege coincided with the possibility of inflicting suffering and humiliation on those below them. It was sought by the frustrated, and this too is a feature which in the microcosm of the Lager reproduces the macrocosm of totalitarian society: in both, without regard to ability and merit, power is generously granted to those willing to pay homage to hierarchic authority, thus attaining an otherwise unattainable social elevation. Finally, it is sought by the many among the oppressed who were contaminated by the oppressors and unconsciously strove to identify with them.

This mimesis, this identification or imitation, or exchange of roles between oppressor and victim, has provoked much discussion. True and invented, disturbing and banal, acute and stupid things have been said: it is not virgin terrain; on the contrary it is a badly ploughed field, trampled and torn up. The film director, Liliana Cavani, who was asked to express briefly the meaning of a beautiful and false film of hers, declared: 'We are all victims or murderers, and we accept these roles voluntarily. Only Sade and Dostoevsky have really understood this'; she also said she believed 'that in every environment, in every relationship, there is a victim–executioner dynamism more or less clearly expressed and generally lived on an unconscious level.'

I am not an expert of the unconscious and the mind's depths, but I do know that few people are experts in this sphere, and that these few are the most cautious; I do not know, and it does not much interest me to know, whether in my depths there lurks a murderer, but I do know that I was a guiltless victim and I was not a murderer. I know that the murderers existed, not only in Germany, and still exist, retired or on active duty, and that to confuse them with their victims is a moral disease or an aesthetic affectation or a sinister sign of complicity; above all, it is precious service rendered (intentionally or not) to the negators of truth. I know that in the Lager, and more generally on the human stage, everything happens, and that therefore the single example proves little. Having said all this quite clearly, and reaffirmed that confusing the two roles means wanting to becloud our need for justice at its foundation, a few more remarks should be made.

It remains true that in the Lager and outside, there exist grey, ambiguous persons, ready to compromise. The extreme pressure of the Lager tends to increase their ranks; they are the rightful owners of a quota of guilt (which grows apace with their freedom of choice), and besides this they are the vectors and instruments of the system's guilt. It remains true that the majority of the oppressors, during or (more often) after their deeds, realised that what they were doing or had done was iniquitous, or perhaps experienced doubts or discomfort, or were even punished; but this suffering is not enough to enrol them among the victims. By the same token, the prisoners' errors and weaknesses are not enough to rank them with their custodians: the prisoners of the Lagers, hundreds of thousands of persons of all social classes, from almost all the countries of Europe, represented an average, unselected sample of humanity. Even if one did not want to take into account the infernal environment into which they had been abruptly flung, it is illogical to demand of them, and it is rhetorical and false to maintain that they all and always followed, the behaviour expected of saints and stoic philosophers. In reality, in the enormous majority of cases, their behaviour was rigidly preordained. In the space of a few weeks or months the deprivations to which they were subjected led them to a condition of pure survival, a daily struggle against hunger, cold, fatigue and blows in which the room for choices (especially moral choices) was reduced to zero; among these, very few survived the test and this thanks to the coming together of many improbable events: in short, they were saved by luck, and there is not much sense in trying to find something common to all their destinies, beyond perhaps their initial good health.

An extreme case of collaboration is represented by the *Sonderkommandos* of Auschwitz and the other extermination camps. Here one hesitates to speak of privilege: whoever belonged to this group was privileged only to the extent that – but at what cost – he had enough to eat for a few months, certainly not because he could be envied. With this duly vague definition, 'Special Squad', the SS referred to the group of prisoners who were entrusted with the running of the crematoria. It was their task to maintain order among the new arrivals (often completely unaware of the destiny awaiting them) who must be sent into the gas chambers; to extract the corpses from the chambers, pull gold teeth from jaws, cut the women's hair, sort and classify clothes, shoes, and the contents of the luggage; transport the bodies to the crematoria and oversee the operation of the ovens; extract and eliminate the ashes. The Special Squad in Auschwitz numbered, depending on the moment, from seven hundred to one thousand active members.

These Special Squads did not escape everyone else's fate; on the contrary, the SS exerted the greatest diligence to prevent any man who had been part of it from surviving and telling. Twelve squads succeeded each other in Auschwitz; each one remained operative for a few months, then it was suppressed, each time with a different trick to head off possible resistance, and as its initiation the next squad burnt the corpses of its predecessors. In October 1944 the last squad rebelled against the SS, blew up one of the crematoria, and was exterminated in an unequal battle which I will discuss later on. The survivors of the Special Squad were therefore very few, having escaped death because of some unforeseeable whim of fate. None of them, after the Liberation, has spoken willingly, and no one speaks willingly about their frightful condition. The information we have about these Squads comes from the meagre depositions of survivors; from the admissions of their 'instigators' tried in various courts; from hints contained in the depositions of German or Polish 'civilians' who, by chance, came into contact with the squads; and lastly, from diary pages which were written feverishly for future memory and buried with extreme care near the crematoria in Auschwitz by some of the squads' members. All these sources are in agreement, and yet we found it difficult, almost impossible, to form an image for ourselves of how these men lived day by day, saw themselves, accepted their condition.

At first, the SS chose them from among the prisoners already registered in the Lager, and it has been testified that the choice was not made only on the basis of physical strength but also by a deep study of the physiognomies. In a few rare cases, the enrolment took place as a punishment. Later on, it was considered preferable to pick out the candidates directly at the railroad platform, on the arrival of each convoy: the SS 'psychologists' noticed that the recruitment was easier if one drew them from among those desperate, disoriented people, exhausted from the journey, bereft of resistance, at the crucial moment of stepping off the train, when every newly arrived person truly felt on the threshold of the darkness and terror of an unearthly space.

The Special Squads were largely made up of Jews. In a certain sense, this is not surprising since the Lager's main purpose was to destroy Jews and, beginning in 1943, the population in Auschwitz was composed of ninety to ninety-five per cent Jews. From another point of view, one is stunned by this paroxysm of perfidiousness and hatred: it must be the Jews who put the Jews into the ovens, it must be shown that the Jews, the sub-race, the sub-men, bow to any and all humiliation, even to destroying themselves. On the other hand, it is proved that not all the SS gladly accepted massacre as a daily task; delegating part of the work to the victims themselves, and indeed the most filthy part, was meant to alleviate (and probably did) a few consciences here and there.

Obviously, it would be iniquitous to attribute such acquiescence to some specifically Jewish peculiarity: members of the Special Squads were also non-Jewish, German and Polish prisoners, although with the 'more dignified' duties of *Kapos*; and also Russian prisoners-of-war, whom the Nazis considered only by one degree superior to the Jews. They were few, because the Russians in Auschwitz were few (they were, for the greater part, exterminated before, immediately after being captured, machine-gunned on the edge of enormous common graves): but they did not behave in a different way from the Jews.

The Special Squads, since they were bearers of a horrendous secret, were kept rigorously apart from the other prisoners and the outside world. Nevertheless, as is known to anyone who had gone through similar experiences, no barrier is ever without a flaw: information, possibly incomplete or distorted, has a tremendous power of penetration, and something always does filter through. Concerning these squads, vague and mangled rumours already circulated among us during our imprisonment, and were confirmed afterwards by the other sources mentioned before, but the intrinsic horror of this human condition has imposed a sort of reserve on all the testimony; so even today it is difficult to conjure up an image of 'what it meant' to be forced to exercise this trade for months. It has been testified that a large amount of alcohol was put at the disposal of those wretches and that they were in a permanent state of complete debasement and prostration. One of them declared: 'Doing this work, one either goes crazy the first day or gets accustomed to it.' Another, though: 'Certainly, I could have killed myself or got myself killed; but I wanted to survive, to avenge myself and bear witness. You mustn't think that we are monsters; we are the same as you, only much more unhappy.'

It is evident that these things which were said, and the innumerable others which were probably said by them and among them but did not reach us, cannot be taken literally. From men who have known such extreme destitution one cannot expect a deposition in the juridical sense of the term, but something that is at once a lament, a curse, an expiation, and an attempt to justify and rehabilitate themselves. One should expect a liberating outburst instead of a Medusa-faced truth.

Conceiving and organising the squads was National Socialism's most demonic crime. Behind the pragmatic aspect (to economise on able men, impose on others the most atrocious tasks), other more subtle aspects can be perceived. This institution represented an attempt to shift on to others – specifically the victims – the burden of guilt, so that they were deprived of even the solace of innocence. It is neither easy nor agreeable to dredge this abyss of viciousness, and yet I think it must be done, because what it was possible to perpetrate yesterday can be attempted again tomorrow, can overwhelm ourselves and our children. One is tempted to turn away with a grimace and close one's mind: this is a temptation one must resist. In fact, the existence of the squads had a meaning, contained a message: 'We, the master race, are your destroyers, but you are no better than we are; if we so wish and we do so wish, we can destroy not only your bodies but also your souls, just as we have destroyed ours.'

Miklos Nyiszli, a Hungarian physician, was one of the very few survivors of the last Special Squad in Auschwitz. He was a renowned anatomical pathologist, expert in autopsies and the chief doctor of the Birkenau SS whose services Mengele – who died a few years ago, escaping justice – had secured; he had given him special treatment and considered him almost as a colleague. Nyiszli was supposed to devote himself in particular to the study of twins: in fact, Birkenau was the only place in the world where it was possible to study the corpses of twins killed at the same moment. Alongside this particular task of his, to which, it should be said in passing, it does not appear he strenuously objected, Nyiszli was also the attending physician of the squad, with which he lived in close contact. Well, he recounts an episode that seems significant to me.

The SS, as I have already said, carefully chose from the Lagers or the arriving convoys the candidates for the squads, and did not hesitate to eliminate on the spot anyone who refused or seemed unsuitable for their duties. The SS treated the newly engaged members with the same contemptuous and detached attitude that they were accustomed to show towards all prisoners and Jews in particular: it had been inculcated in them that these were despicable beings, enemies of Germany, and therefore not entitled to life; and in the most favourable instance, they should be compelled to work until they died of exhaustion. But this is not how they behaved with the veterans of the squad: in them, they recognised, to some extent, colleagues, by now as inhuman as themselves, hitched to the same cart, bound together by the foul link of imposed complicity. So, Nyiszli tells how during a 'work' pause he attended a soccer game between the SS and the SK (*Sonderkommando*), that is to say, between a group representing the SS on guard at the crematorium and a group representing the Special Squad. Other men of the SS and the rest of the squad are present at the game; they take sides, bet, applaud, urge the players on as if, rather than at the gates of hell, the game were taking place on the village green.

Nothing of this kind ever took place, nor would it have been conceivable, with other categories of prisoners; but with them, with the 'crematorium ravens', the SS could enter the field on an equal footing, or almost. Behind this armistice one hears Satanic laughter: it is consummated, we have succeeded, you are no longer the other race, the anti-race, the prime enemy of the millennial Reich: you are no longer the people who reject idols. We have embraced you, corrupted you, dragged you to the bottom with us. You are like us, you proud people, dirtied with your own blood, as we are. You too, like us and like Cain, have killed the brother. Come, we can play together.

Nyiszli describes another episode that deserves to be meditated upon. In the gas chamber have been jammed together and murdered the components of a recently arrived convoy and the squad is performing its horrendous everyday work, sorting out the tangle of corpses, washing them with hoses and transporting them to the crematorium, but on the floor they find a young woman who is still alive. The event is exceptional, unique; perhaps the human bodies formed a barrier around her, sequestered a pocket of air that remained breathable. The men are perplexed; death is their trade at all hours, death is a habit because, precisely, 'one either goes crazy the first day or gets accustomed to it', but this woman is alive. They hide her, warm her, bring her beef broth, question her: the girl is sixteen years old, she cannot orient herself in space or time, does not know where she is, has gone through, without understanding it, the sequence of the sealed train, the brutal preliminary selection, the stripping, the entry into the chamber from which no one had ever come out alive. She has not understood, but she has seen; therefore she must die, and the men of the squad know it just as they know that they too must die for the same reason. But these slaves, debased by alcohol and the daily slaughter, are transformed; they no longer have before them the anonymous mass, the flood of frightened, stunned people coming off the boxcars: they have a person.

One cannot help but think of the 'unusual respect' and the hesitation of the 'foul Monatto' when faced by the individual case, faced by the child Cecilia killed by the plague whom, in Manzoni's novel *The Betrothed*, the mother refuses to let be flung on the cart together with the heaped-up corpses. Occurrences like this astonish because they conflict with the image we have of man in harmony with himself, coherent, monolithic; and they should not astonish because that is not how man is. Compassion and brutality can coexist in the same individual and in the same moment, despite all logic; and for all that, compassion itself eludes logic. There is no proportion between the pity we feel and the extent of the pain by which the pity is aroused: a single Anne Frank excites more emotion than the myriads who suffered as she did but whose image has remained in the shadows. Perhaps it is necessary that it can be so; if we had to and were able to suffer the sufferings of every-one, we could not live. Perhaps the dreadful gift of pity for the many is granted only to saints; to the Monatti, to the members of the Special Squad, and to all of us there remains in the best of cases, only the sporadic pity addressed to the single individual, the *Mitmensch*, the co-man: the human being of flesh and blood standing before us, within the reach of our providentially myopic senses.

A doctor is called, and he revives the girl with an injection: yes, the gas has not had its effect, she will be able to survive, but where and how? Just then Muhsfeld arrives; he is one of the SS men attached to the death installations. The doctor calls him to one side and presents the case to him. Muhsfeld hesitates, then he decides: no, the girl must die; if she were older, it would be a different matter, she would have more sense, perhaps she could be convinced to keep quiet about what has happened to her, but she's only sixteen: she can't be trusted. And yet, he does not kill her with his own hands; he calls one of his underlings to eliminate her with a blow to the nape of the neck. Now, this man Muhsfeld was not a compassionate person; his daily ration of slaughter was studded with arbitrary and capricious acts, marked by his inventions of refined cruelty. He was tried in 1947 in Cracow, sentenced to death and hanged and this was right; but not even he was a monolith. If he had lived in a different environment and epoch, it is likely that he would have behaved like any other common man.

In *The Brothers Karamazov* Grushenka tells the fable of the little onion. A vicious old woman dies and goes to hell, but her guardian angel, squeezing his memory, recalls that she once, only once, gave a beggar the gift of a little onion she had dug up from her garden: he holds the little onion out to her, and the old woman grasps it and is lifted out of the flames of hell. This fable has always struck me as revolting: what human monster did not throughout his life make the gift of a little onion, if not to others, to his children, his wife, his dog? That single, immediately erased instant of pity is certainly not enough to absolve Muhsfeld. It is enough, however, to place him too, though at its extreme boundary, within the grey band, that zone of ambiguity which irradiates around regimes based on terror and obsequiousness.

It is not difficult to judge Muhsfeld, and I do not believe that the tribunal which sentenced him had any doubts; on the other hand, in contrast to this, our need and our ability to judge falters when confronted by the Special Squads. Questions immediately arise, convulsed questions for which it is an arduous task to find an answer that will reassure us about man's nature. Why did they accept that task? Why didn't they rebel? Why didn't they prefer death?

To a certain extent, the facts available to us permit us to attempt to answer. Not all did accept; some did rebel, knowing they would die. Concerning at least one case we have precise information: a group of four hundred Jews from Corfu, who in July 1944 had been included in the squad, refused without exception to do the work and was immediately killed by gas. There has remained the memory of various individual mutinies, all immediately punished by an atrocious death (Filip Müller, one of the very few survivors of the squads, tells of a companion of his whom the SS pushed into the oven alive), and many cases of suicide at the moment of recruitment, or immediately after. Finally, it must be remembered that it was precisely the Special Squad which in October 1944 organised the only desperate attempt at revolt in the history of the Auschwitz Lager, which we have already mentioned.

The information about this exploit which has come down to us is neither complete nor without contradictions. It is known that the insurgents (the personnel of two of the five Auschwitz-Birkenau crematoria), poorly armed and without contacts with the Polish Partisans outside the Lager and the clandestine defence organisation inside the Lager, blew up crematorium number three and engaged the SS in battle. The battle was soon over; a number of the insurgents managed to cut the barbed wire and escape to the outside but were captured soon afterwards. Not one of them survived; approximately four hundred and fifty were killed immediately by the SS; among the latter, three were killed and twelve wounded.

Those whom we know about, the miserable manual labourers of the slaughter, are therefore the others, those who from one shift to the next preferred a few more weeks of life (what a life!) to immediate death, but who in no instance induced themselves, or were induced, to kill with their own hands. I repeat: I believe that no one is authorised to judge them, not those who lived through the experience of the Lager and even less those who did not live through it. I would invite anyone who dares pass judgement to carry out upon himself, with sincerity, a conceptual experiment: let him imagine, if he can, that he has lived for months or years in a ghetto, tormented by chronic hunger, fatigue, promiscuity and humiliation; that he has seen die around him, one by one, his beloved; that he is cut off from the world, unable to receive or transmit news; that, finally, he is loaded on to a train, eighty or a hundred persons to a boxcar; that he travels towards the unknown, blindly, for sleepless days and nights; and that he is at last flung inside the walls of an indecipherable inferno. This, it seems to me, is the true *Befehlnotstand*, the 'state of compulsion following an order': not the one systematically and impudently invoked by the Nazis dragged to judgement, and later on (but in their footsteps) by the war criminals of many other countries. The former is a rigid either/or, immediate obedience or death; the latter is an internal fact at the centre of power and could have been resolved (actually often was resolved) by some manoeuvre, some slow-down in career, moderate punishment or, in the worst of cases, the objector's transfer to the front.

The experiment I have proposed is not pleasant; Vercors tried to describe it in his story *Les armes de la Nuit* (Albin Michel, Paris, 1953), in which he speaks of 'the death of the soul', and which reread today seems to me intolerably infected by aestheticism and literary lechery. But it is doubtless true that it deals with the death of the soul. Now, nobody can know for how long and under what trials his soul can resist before yielding or breaking. Every human being possesses a reserve of strength whose extent is unknown to him: it can be large, small, or non-existent, and only extreme adversity makes it possible to evaluate it. Even without having recourse to the extreme case of the Special Squads, it often happens to us who have returned that when we describe our vicissitudes, our interlocutor will say: 'In your place I would not have lasted for a single day.' This statement does not have a precise meaning: one is never in another's place. Each individual is so complex an object that there is no point in trying to foresee his behaviour, all the more so in extreme situations; and neither is it possible to foresee one's own behaviour. Therefore, I ask that we meditate on the story of 'the crematorium ravens' with pity and rigour, but that a judgement of them be suspended.

The same *impotentia judicandi* paralyses us when confronted by the Rumkowski case. The story of Chaim Rumkowski is not exactly a Lager story, although it reaches its conclusion in the Lager: it is a ghetto story, but so eloquent on the fundamental theme of human ambiguity fatally provoked by oppression that I would say it fits our discourse only too well. I repeat it here, even though I have already told it elsewhere.* On my return from Auschwitz I found in my pocket a curious coin of light alloy, which I have saved to this day. It is scratched and corroded; on one side it has the Hebrew star (the 'shield of David'), the date 1943, and the word *getto*; on the other side it has the inscription *Quittung über 10 Mark* and *Der Älteste der Juden in Litzmannstadt*, that is, respectively, 'Receipt for ten marks' and 'The elder of the Jews in Litzmannstadt': in short, it was a coin for internal use in a ghetto. For many years I forgot about its existence, and then, around 1974, I was able to reconstruct its story, which is fascinating and sinister.

In honour of a certain General Litzmann who had defeated

* In *Moments of Reprieve* (Michael Joseph, London, 1986).

the Russians during the First World War, the Nazis had re-baptised the Polish city of Lodz with the name of Litzmannstadt. During the final months of 1944, the last survivors of the Lodz ghetto were deported to Auschwitz: I probably found that by now useless coin on the ground in the Lager.

In 1939 Lodz had 750,000 inhabitants and was the most industrialised Polish city, the most 'modern' and the ugliest: it made its living from the textile industry, like Manchester and Biella, and it was conditioned by the presence of a myriad of small and large factories, which were mostly antiquated even then. As in all cities of a certain importance in occupied Eastern Europe, the Nazis hastened to set up a ghetto in it, reinstating, aggravated by their modern ferocity, the regime of the medieval and Counter-Reformation ghettos. The Lodz ghetto, begun as early as February 1940, was first in order of time, and after that of Warsaw second in the number of inhabitants: it grew to more than 160,000 Jews and was disbanded only in the autumn of 1944. So it was the longest lived of the Nazi ghettos, and this must be attributed to two reasons: its economic importance and the perplexing personality of its president.

His name was Chaim Rumkowski. Formerly a failed small industrialist, after varied travels and uneven fortunes he had settled in Lodz in 1917. In 1940 he was almost sixty and a widower without children; he enjoyed a certain esteem, and was known as the director of Jewish charities and as an energetic, uncultivated and authoritarian man. The position of President (or Elder) of a ghetto was intrinsically frightful, but it was a position, it constituted social recognition, raised one a step up the ladder and conferred rights and privileges, that is, authority: and Rumkowski passionately loved authority. How he happened to obtain the investiture is not known: perhaps it was simply a hoax in the sinister Nazi style (Rumkowski was, or seemed to be, a fool with an air of respectability – in short, the ideal dupe); perhaps he himself had intrigued to be chosen, so strong in him must have been the will to power.

It is proved that the four years of his presidency or, more exactly, his dictatorship, were an astonishing tangle of megalomaniac dream, barbaric vitality, and real diplomatic and organisational skill. He soon came to see himself in the role of absolute but enlightened monarch, and he was certainly encouraged along this path by his German masters who, true enough, played with him, but appreciated his talents as a good administrator and man of order. He obtained from them the authorisation to mint money, both metallic (that coin of mine) and on watermarked paper which was officially supplied him. This currency was used to pay the worn-out workers in the ghettos; they could spend it in the ghetto stores to acquire their food rations, which on the average amounted to 800 calories a day. (Let me mention in passing that at least 2,000 calories are needed to survive in a condition of total repose.)

From these famished citizens of his, Rumkowski aspired to obtain not only obedience and respect but also love: in this respect, modern dictatorships differ from the ancient ones. Since he disposed of an army of excellent artists and craftsmen, ready to perform at his slightest hint in exchange for a quarter-loaf of bread, he gave orders to design and print stamps bearing his effigy, with his snow-white hair and beard haloed by the light of Hope and Faith. He had a carriage drawn by a skeleton nag and in it he rode through the streets of his minuscule kingdom, streets crowded with beggars and postulants. He had a regal mantle, and surrounded himself with a court of flat-terers and henchmen; he had his courtier-poets compose hymns in which 'his firm and powerful hands' were celebrated, and the peace and order which, thanks to him, reigned in the ghetto. He ordered that the children in the nefarious schools, devastated daily by epidemics, malnutrition and German raids, should be given the assignment to write essays in praise 'of our beloved and providential President'. Like all autocrats, he hastened to organise an efficient police force, ostensibly to maintain order, but in fact to protect his own person and impose his discipline. It was composed of 600 guards armed with clubs and an unspecified number of spies. He delivered many speeches, some of which have been preserved for us and whose style is unmistakable: he had adopted the oratorical technique of Mussolini and Hitler, the style of inspired recitation, pseudo-colloquy with the crowd, the creation of consent through subjugation and plaudit. Perhaps this imitation of his was deliberate; perhaps, instead, it was unconscious identification with the model of the 'necessary hero' who at the time dominated Europe and was sung by d'Annunzio; but it is more likely that his attitude sprang from his condition as a small tyrant, impotent with those above him and omnipotent with those below him. The man who has throne and sceptre, who is not afraid of being contradicted or derided, speaks like this.

And yet his figure was more complex than it may appear thus far. Rumkowski was not only a renegade and an accomplice; to some extent, besides convincing others, he must have progressively convinced himself that he *was* a Messiah, a saviour of his people, whose welfare, at least at intervals, he must certainly have desired. One must benefit in order to feel beneficent, and feeling beneficent is gratifying even for a corrupt satrap. Paradoxically, his identification with the oppressor alternates, or goes hand in hand, with an identification with the oppressed, because, as Thomas Mann says, man is a mixed-up creature; and he becomes all the more confused, we might add, the more he is subjected to tensions: at that point he evades our judgement, just as a compass goes wild at the magnetic pole.

Even though he was constantly despised and derided by the Germans, it is probable that Rumkowski thought of himself not as a servant but as a Lord. He must have taken his own authority seriously: when the Gestapo, without warning, seized *his* councilmen, he came courageously to their rescue, exposing himself to jeers and slaps which he knew how to endure with dignity. On other occasions, he tried to bargain with the Germans who kept exacting more and more cloth from Lodz and from him ever more numerous contingents of useless mouths (children, old and sick people) to send to the gas chamber in Treblinka and, later on, Auschwitz. The very harshness with which he hastened to repress signs of insubordination on the part of his subjects (there existed in Lodz, as in other ghettos, nuclei of bold political resistance, with Zionist, Bundist, or Communist roots) did not originate so much in servility towards the Germans, as in *lèse-majesté*, indignation over the outrage inflicted on his regal person.

In September 1944, as the Russian front approached, the Nazis initiated the liquidation of the Lodz ghetto. Men and women by the tens of thousands were deported to Auschwitz, *anus mundi*, ultimate drainage site of the German universe; worn out as they were, they were all eliminated almost immediately. About a thousand men remained in the ghetto, to dismantle the machinery of the factories and cancel the traces of the slaughter: they were liberated by the Red Army shortly afterwards, and it is to them that we owe the information recorded here.

About Chaim Rumkowski's final fate two versions exist, as though the ambiguity under whose sign he lived was protracted to envelop his death. According to the first version, in the course of the ghetto's liquidation, he supposedly tried to oppose the deportation of his brother, from whom he did not want to be separated. A German officer then, it is said, proposed he should leave voluntarily with his brother, and he is supposed to have accepted. Another version claims instead that Rumkowski's rescue was attempted by Hans Biebow, another figure drenched in duplicity.

This shady German industrialist was the functionary responsible for the ghetto's administration and at the same time its exclusive contractor: hence his was a delicate position, because the textile factories in Lodz worked for the armed forces. Biebow was not a ferocious beast; he was not interested in creating useless suffering or punishing the Jews for the sin of being Jewish, but he was interested in profiting from his contracts, in both legitimate and other ways. The torment in the ghetto touched him, but only indirectly; he wanted the slave workers to work, and therefore he did not want them to die of hunger: his moral sense ended there. In reality, he was the true master of the ghetto, and he was linked to Rumkowski by that buyer–supplier relationship which often becomes a crude friendship. Biebow, a small jackal too cynical to take race demonology seriously, would have liked to put off forever the dismantling of the ghetto, which, for him, was an excellent business deal, and to preserve Rumkowski from deportation, on whose complicity he relied. Here one sees how often a realist is objectively better than a theoretician. But the theoreticians of the SS thought otherwise, and they were the stronger. They were *grundlich* radicals: get rid of the ghetto and get rid of Rumkowski.

Unable to deal with the matter otherwise, Biebow, who had good connections, handed Rumkowski a letter addressed to the Lager of his destination, and guaranteed that it would protect him and assure him special treatment. Rumkowski supposedly asked and obtained from Biebow the right to travel to Auschwitz – he and his family – with the decorum becoming his rank, that is, in a special car, attached to the end of a convoy of freight cars packed with deportees without privileges: there was only one fate for Jews in German hands, whether they were cowards or heroes, humble or proud. Neither the letter nor the special carriage were able to save Chaim Rumkowski, the king of the Jews, from the gas chamber.

A story like this is not self-enclosed. It is pregnant, full of significance, asks more questions than it answers, sums up in itself the entire theme of the grey zone and leaves one dangling. It shouts and clamours to be understood, because in it one perceives a symbol, as in dreams and the signs of heaven.

Who is Rumkowski? He is not a monster, neither is he a common man; yet many around us are like him. The failures that preceded his 'career' are significant: few are the men who draw moral strength from failure. It seems to me that in his story it is possible to recognise in an exemplary form the almost physical necessity which causes the ill-defined area of ambiguity and compromise to be born from political coercion. At the foot of every absolute throne, men such as Rumkowski crowd in order to grasp their small portion of power. It is a recurrent spectacle. We remember the deadly struggles during the last months of the Second World War in Hitler's court and among the ministers of Mussolini's Republic of Salò; grey men, blind first and criminal later, frenziedly dividing among themselves the tatters of an iniquitous and moribund authority.

Power is like a drug: the need for either is unknown to anyone who has not tried them, but after the initiation, which (as for Rumkowski) can be fortuitous, the dependency and need for ever larger doses is born; also born is the denial of reality and the return to childish dreams of omnipotence. If the interpretation of a Rumkowski intoxicated with power is valid, it must be admitted that the intoxication occurred not because of, but rather despite, the ghetto environment; that is, it is so powerful as to prevail even under conditions that would seem to be designed to extinguish all individual will. In fact, in him as in his more famous models, the syndrome produced by protracted and undisputed power is clearly visible: a distorted view of the world, dogmatic arrogance, need for adulation, convulsive clinging to the levers of command, and contempt for the law.

All this does not exonerate Rumkowski from his responsibilities. That a Rumkowski should have emerged from Lodz's affliction is painful and distressing; if he had survived his own tragedy, and the tragedy of the ghetto which he contaminated, superimposing on it his histrionic image, no tribunal would have absolved him, nor certainly can we absolve him on the moral plane. But there are extenuating circumstances: an infernal order such as National Socialism was, exercises a frightful power of corruption, against which it is difficult to guard oneself. It degrades its victims and makes them similar to itself, because it needs both great and small complicities. To resist it a truly solid moral armature is needed, and the one available to Chaim Rumkowski, the Lodz merchant, together with his entire generation, was fragile. But how strong is ours, the Europeans of today? How would each of us behave if driven by necessity and at the same time lured by seduction?

Rumkowski's story is the sorry, disquieting story of the *Kapos* and Lager functionaries; the small hierarchs who serve a regime to whose misdeeds they are willingly blind; of the subordinates who sign everything because a signature costs little; of those who shake their heads but acquiesce; those who say, 'If I did not do it, someone else worse than I would.'

Rumkowski, a symbolic and compendiary figure, must be placed in this band of half-consciences. Whether high or low it is difficult to say: only he could clarify this if he could speak before us, even lying, as perhaps he always lied, to himself also; he would in any case help us understand him, as every defendant helps his judge, even though he does not want to, even if he lies, because man's capacity to play a role is not unlimited.

But all this is not enough to explain the sense of urgency and threat that emanates from this story. Perhaps its meaning is vaster. We are all mirrored in Rumkowski, his ambiguity is ours, it is our second nature, we hybrids moulded from clay and spirit; his fever is ours, the fever of our Western civilisation that 'descends into hell with trumpets and drums', and its miserable adornments are the distorting image of our symbols of social prestige. His folly is that of presumptuousness and mortal Man as he is described by Isabella in *Measure for Measure*, the Man who,

> Dressed in a little brief authority,
> Most ignorant of what he's most assured,
> His glassy essence, like an angry ape,
> Plays such fantastic tricks before high heaven
> As make the angels weep . . .

Like Rumkowski, we too are so dazzled by power and

prestige as to forget our essential fragility: willingly or not we come to terms with power, forgetting that we are all in the ghetto, that the ghetto is walled in, that outside the ghetto reign the lords of death and that close by the train is waiting.

# CHAPTER THREE

# Shame

There exists a sterotyped picture, proposed innumerable times, consecrated by literature and poetry and picked up by the cinema: at the end of the storm, when 'the quiet after the storm' arrives, all hearts rejoice. 'To be freed from pain is delightful for us.' After the disease, health returns; to deliver us from imprisonment 'our boys' arrive just in time, the liberators, with waving flags; the soldier returns and again finds his family and peace.

Judging by the stories told by many who came back and from my own memories, Leopardi the pessimist went beyond truth in this representation: despite himself, he showed himself to be an optimist. In the majority of cases, the hour of liberation was neither joyful nor lighthearted: for most it occurred against a tragic background of destruction, slaughter and suffering. In that moment in which they felt they were again becoming men (that is, responsible), the sorrows of men returned: the sorrow of the dispersed or lost family; the universal suffering all around; their own exhaustion, which seemed definitive, no longer curable; the problems of a life to begin all over again amid the rubble, often alone. Not 'pleasure the son of misery': misery the son of misery. Leaving pain behind was a delight only for a few fortunate beings, or only for a few instants, or for very simple souls; almost always it coincided with a phase of anguish.

Anguish is known to everyone since childhood, and everyone knows that it is often blank, undifferentiated. It rarely carries a clearly written label that also contains its motivation; when it does have one, it is often mendacious. One can believe or declare oneself to be anguished for one reason and be so due to something totally different: one can think that one is suffering at facing the future and instead be suffering because of one's past; one can think that one is suffering for others, out of pity, out of compassion, and instead be suffering for one's own reasons, more or less profound, more or less avowable and avowed; sometimes so deep that only the specialist, the analyst of souls, knows how to exhume them.

Naturally, I dare not maintain that the movie script I referred to before is false in every case. Many liberations were experienced with full, authentic joy: above all by combatants, both military and political, who at that moment saw the aspirations of their militancy and their lives realised; and also on the part of those who had suffered less and for less time, or only in their own person and not because of their family, friends, or loved ones. And besides, luckily, human beings are not all the same: there are among us those who have the virtue and the privilege of extracting, isolating those instants of happiness, of enjoying them fully as though they were extracting pure gold from the dross. And finally, among the testimonies, written or heard, there are also those that are unconsciously stylised, in which convention prevails over genuine memory: 'whoever is freed from slavery rejoices. I too was liberated, hence I too rejoice over it. In all films, all novels, just as in *Fidelio* the shattering of the chains is a moment of solemn or fervid jubilation, and so was mine.' This is a specific case of that drifting of memory I mentioned in the first chapter, and which is accentuated with the passing of years and the piling up of the experiences of others, true or presumed, on the layer of one's own. But anyone who, purportedly or by temperament, shuns rhetoric, usually speaks in a different voice. This for example is how, in the last page of his memoir *Eyewitness Auschwitz – Three Years in the Gas Chambers*, his liberation is described by Filip Müller, whose experience was much more terrible than mine:

Although it may seem incredible, I experienced a complete

letdown or depression. That moment, on which for three years all my thoughts and my secret desires were concentrated, did not arouse in me happiness or any other feeling. I let myself fall from my pallet and crawled to the door. Once I was outside I tried in vain to go further, then I simply lay down on the ground in the woods and fell asleep.

I now reread the passage from my own book, *The Truce* which was published in Italy only in 1963, although I had written these words as early as 1947. In it is a description of the first Russian soldiers facing our Lager packed with corpses and dying persons.

They did not greet us, nor smile; they seemed oppressed, not only by pity but also by a confused restraint which sealed their mouths, and kept their eyes fastened on the funereal scene. It was the same shame which we knew so well, which submerged us after the selections, and every time we had to witness or undergo an outrage: the shame that the Germans never knew, the shame which the just man experiences when confronted by a crime committed by another, and he feels remorse because of its existence, because of its having been irrevocably introduced into the world of existing things, and because his will has proven nonexistent or feeble and was incapable of putting up a good defence.

I do not think that there is anything I need erase or correct, but there is something I must add. That many (and myself) experienced 'shame', that is, a feeling of guilt during the imprisonment and afterwards is an ascertained fact confirmed by numerous testimonies. It may seem absurd, but it does exist. I will try to interpret it myself, and to comment on the interpretations of others.

As I mentioned at the start, the vague discomfort which accompanied liberation was not precisely shame, but as such it was perceived. Why? There are various explanations one can present.

From this examination I will exclude certain exceptional cases: the prisoners who, almost all of them political, had the strength and possibility to act within the Lager in defence of and to the advantage of their companions. We, the almost total majority of common prisoners, did not know about them, and did not even suspect their existence: which is logical because, due to obvious political and police necessity (the Political Section of Auschwitz was simply a branch of the Gestapo) they were forced to operate secretly, not only where the Germans were concerned, but in regard to everyone. In Auschwitz, the concentrationary empire which in my time was constituted by ninety-five per cent Jews, this political network was embryonic; I witnessed only one episode that should have led me to sense something if I had not been crushed by the everyday travail.

Around May 1944 our almost innocuous *Kapo* was replaced, and the newcomer proved to be a fearsome individual. All *Kapos* gave beatings: this was an obvious part of their duties, it was their more or less accepted language; after all, it was the only language that could truly be understood by everyone in that perpetual Babel. In its various nuances, it was understood as an incitement to work, a warning or punishment, and in the hierarchy of suffering it had a low rank. Now, the new *Kapo* gave his beatings in a different way, in a convulsive, malicious, perverse way: on the nose, the shin, the genitals. He beat to hurt, to produce suffering and humiliation. Not even, as many others, out of blind racial hatred, but with the obvious intention of inflicting pain, indiscriminately, and without a pretext, on all his subjects. It is probable that he was a mental case, but it is clear that under those conditions, the indulgence that we today consider obligatory towards such sick people would have been out of place there. I spoke about it with a colleague, a Jewish Croatian Communist: what should we do? how protect ourselves? act collectively? He gave me a strange smile and simply said: 'You'll see, he won't last long.' In fact, the beater vanished within a week.

But years later, during a meeting of survivors, I found out that some political prisoners attached to the Work Office inside the camp had the terrifying power of switching the registration numbers on the lists of prisoners destined to be gassed. Anyone who had the ability and will to act in this way, to oppose in this or other ways the machine of the Lager, was beyond the reach of 'shame': or at least the shame of which I am speaking, perhaps because he experiences something else. Equally protected must have been Sivadjan, a silent and tranquil man whom I mentioned in passing in *If This Is A Man*, in the chapter 'The Canto of Ulysses', and about whom I discovered on that same occasion that he had brought explosives into the camp to foment a possible insurrection.

In my opinion, the feeling of shame or guilt that coincided with reacquired freedom was extremely composite: it contained diverse elements, and in diverse proportions for each individual. It must be remembered that each of us, both objectively and subjectively, lived the Lager in his own way.

Coming out of the darkness, one suffered because of the reacquired consciousness of having been diminished. Not by our will, cowardice, or fault, yet nevertheless we had lived for months and years at an animal level: our days were encumbered from dawn to nightfall by hunger, fatigue, cold, fear, and a space for reflection, reasoning, experiencing emotions was wiped out. We endured filth, promiscuity, and destitution, suffering much less than we would have suffered from such things in normal life, because our moral yardstick was changed. Furthermore, all of us had stolen: in the kitchen, the factory, the camp, in short, 'from the others', from the opposing side, but it was theft nevertheless; some (few) had fallen so low as to steal bread from their own companions. We had not only forgotten our country and our culture, but also our family, our past, the future we had imagined for ourselves, because, like animals, we were confined to the present moment. Only at rare intervals did we come out of this condition of levelling, during the very few Sundays of rest, the fleeting minutes before falling asleep, or the fury of the air raids, but these were painful moments precisely because they gave us the opportunity to measure our diminishment from the outside.

I believe that it is precisely due to this turning to look back at the 'perilous water' that so many suicides occurred after (sometimes immediately after) the liberation. It was in any case a critical moment which coincided with a flood of rethinking and depression. By contrast, all historians of the Lager – and also of the Soviet camps – agree in pointing out that cases of suicide *during* imprisonment were rare. Several explanations of this fact have been put forward; for my part I offer three, which are not mutually exclusive.

First of all, suicide is an act of man and not of the animal; it is a meditated act, a non-instinctive, unnatural choice; and in the Lager there were few opportunities to choose – one lived precisely like enslaved animals that sometimes let themselves die but do not kill themselves. Secondly: 'there were other things to think about', as the saying goes. The day was dense: one had to think about satisfying hunger, in some way elude fatigue and cold, avoid the blows; precisely because of the constant imminence of death there was no time to concentrate on the idea of death. Svevo's remark in *The Confessions of Zeno* has the rawness of truth, when he ruthlessly describes his father's agony: 'When one is dying, one is much too busy to think about death. All one's organism is devoted to breathing.' Thirdly, in the majority of cases, suicide is born from a feeling of guilt that no punishment has attenuated; now, the harshness of imprisonment was perceived as punishment, and the feeling of guilt (if there is punishment, there must have been guilt) was relegated to the background only to re-emerge after the liberation: in other words, there was no need to punish oneself by suicide because of a (true or presumed) guilt, one was already expiating it by one's daily suffering.

What guilt? When all was over, the awareness emerged that we had not done anything, or not enough, against the system into which we had been absorbed. About the failed resistance in the Lagers or, more accurately, in some Lagers, too much has been said, too superficially, above all by people who had altogether different crimes to account for. Anyone who made the attempt knows that there existed situations, collective or personal, in which active resistance was possible; and others, much more frequent, in which it was not. It is known that especially in 1941 millions of Soviet military prisoners fell into German hands. They were young, generally well nourished and robust, they had military and political training, often they formed organic units with soldiers with the rank of corporal and up, non-commissioned officers and officers; they hated the Germans who had invaded their country; and yet they rarely resisted. Malnutrition, despoilment, and other physical discomforts which it is so easy and economically advantageous to provoke and at which the Nazis were masters, are rapidly destructive and paralyse before destroying; all the more when they are preceded by years of segregation, humiliations, maltreatments, forced migrations, the laceration of family ties, the rupture of contact with the rest of the world. Now, this was the situation of the bulk of the prisoners who had landed in Auschwitz after the introductory hell of the ghettos or the collection camps.

Therefore, on a rational plane, there should not have been much to be ashamed of, but shame persisted nevertheless, especially for the few, bright examples of those who had the strength and possibility to resist. I spoke about this in the chapter entitled 'The Last' in *If This Is A Man*, where I described the public hanging of a resistor before the terrified and apathetic crowd of prisoners. This is a thought that then just barely grazed us, but which returned 'afterwards': you too could have, you certainly should have; and this is a judgement that the survivor believes he sees in the eyes of those (especially the young) who listen to his stories, and judge with facile hindsight; or who perhaps feel cruelly repelled. Consciously or not, he feels accused and judged, compelled to justify and defend himself.

Self-accusation is more realistic, or the accusation of having failed in terms of human solidarity. Few survivors feel guilty about having deliberately damaged, robbed, or beaten a companion: those who did so (the *Kapos*, but not only they) block out the memory; but by contrast, almost everybody feels guilty of having omitted to offer help. The presence at your side of a companion who is weaker, or less cunning, or older, or too young, hounding you with his demands for help or with his simply being there, which is itself an entreaty, is a constant in the life of the Lager. The demand for solidarity, for a human word, advice, even only a listening ear, was permanent and universal but rarely satisfied. There was no time, space, privacy, patience, strength; most often, the person to whom the request was addressed in turn found himself in a state of need, of credit.

I remember with a certain relief that I once tried to give courage (at a moment when I felt I had some) to an eighteen-year-old Italian who had just arrived, who was floundering in the bottomless despair of his first days in the camp: I forget what I told him, certainly words of hope, perhaps a few lies, acceptable to a 'new arrival', expressed with the authority of my twenty-five years and my three months of seniority; at any rate, I made him the gift of a momentary attention. But I also remember, with disquiet, that much more often I shrugged my shoulders impatiently at other requests, and this precisely when I had been in camp for almost a year and so had accumulated a good store of experience: but I had also deeply assimilated the principal rule of the place, which made it mandatory that you should first of all take care of yourself. I never found this rule expressed with as much frankness as in the book entitled *Prisoners of Fear* by Ella Lingens-Reiner (where, however, the sentences are attributed to a woman doctor who, disregarding her own statement, proved to be generous and brave and saved many lives):

How was I able to survive in Auschwitz? My principle is: I come first, second and third. Then nothing, then again I; and then all the others.

In the August of 1944 it was very hot in Auschwitz. A torrid, tropical wind lifted clouds of dust from the buildings wrecked by the air raids, dried the sweat on our skin, and thickened the blood in our veins. My squad had been sent into a cellar to clear out the plaster rubble, and we all suffered from thirst: a new suffering, which was added to, indeed, multiplied by the old one of hunger. There was no drinkable water in the camp or often on the work site; in those days there was often no water in the wash trough either, undrinkable but good enough to freshen up and clean off the dust. As a rule, the evening soup and the ersatz coffee distributed around ten o'clock were abundantly sufficient to quench our thirst; but now they were no longer enough and thirst tormented us. It is more imperative than hunger: hunger obeys the nerves, grants remission, can be temporarily obliterated by an emotion, a pain, a fear (we had realised this during our journey by train from Italy); not so with thirst, which does not give respite. Hunger exhausts, thirst enrages; in those days it accompanied us day and night: by day, on the work site, whose order (our enemy, but nevertheless order, a place of logic and certainty) was transformed into a chaos of shattered constructions; by night, in the hut without ventilation, as we gasped the air breathed a hundred times before.

The corner of the cellar that had been assigned to me by the *Kapo* and where I was to remove the rubble was next to a large room filled with chemical equipment in the process of being installed but already damaged by the bombs. Along the vertical wall ran a two-inch pipe, which ended in a spigot just above the floor. A water pipe? I took a chance and tried to open it. I was alone, nobody saw me. It was blocked, but using a stone for a hammer I managed to shift it a few milli- metres. A few drops came out; they had no odour. I caught them on my fingers: it really seemed water. I had no recep- tacle; the drops came out slowly, without pressure: the pipe must be only half full, perhaps less. I stretched out on the floor with my mouth under the spigot, without trying to open it further: it was water made tepid by the sun, insipid, perhaps distilled or the result of condensation; at any rate, a delight.

How much water can a two-inch-wide pipe one or two metres high contain? A litre, perhaps not even that. I could drink all of it immediately, it would have been the safest way. Or save a bit for the next day. Or share half of it with Alberto. Or reveal the secret to the whole squad. I chose the third path, that of selfishness extended to the one who is closest to you, which in distant times a friend of mine appropriately called us-ism. We drank all the water, in small, avaricious gulps, changing places under the spigot, only the two of us. On the sly; but on the march back to camp at my side I found Daniele, all grey with cement dust, his lips cracked and his eyes feverish, and I felt guilty. I exchanged a look with Alberto, we understood each other immediately and hoped nobody had seen us. But Daniele had caught a glimpse of us in that strange position, supine near the wall among the rubble, and had suspected something, and then had guessed. He curtly told me so many months later, in White Russia, after the liberation: why the two of you and not I? It was the 'civilian' moral code surfacing again. The same according to which I the free man of today perceive as horrifying the death sentence of the sadistic *Kapo*, decided upon and executed without appeal, silently, with the stroke of an eraser. Is this belated shame justified or not? I was not able to decide then and I am not able to decide even now, but shame was there and is there, concrete, heavy, perennial. Daniele is dead now, but in our meetings as survivors, fraternal, affectionate, the veil of that act of omission, that unshared glass of water, stood between us, transparent, not expressed, but perceptible and 'costly'.

Changing moral codes is always costly: all heretics, apostates, and dissidents know this. We cannot judge our behaviour or that of others, driven at that time by the code of that time, on the basis of today's code; but the anger that pervades us when one of the 'others' feels entitled to consider us 'apostates' or, more precisely, reconverted, seems right to me.

Are you ashamed because you are alive in place of another? And in particular, of a man more generous, more sensitive, wiser, more useful, more worthy of living than you? You cannot exclude this: you examine yourself, you review your memories, hoping to find them all, and that none of them are masked or disguised; no, you find no obvious transgressions, you did not usurp anyone's place, you did not beat anyone (but would you have had the strength to do so?), you did not accept positions (but none were offered to you . . .), you did not steal anyone's bread; nevertheless, you cannot exclude it. It is no more than a supposition, indeed the shadow of a suspicion; that everyone is his brother's Cain, that everyone of us (but this time I say 'us' in a much vaster, indeed universal sense) has usurped his neighbour's place and lived in his stead. It is a supposition, but it gnaws at us; it has nestled deeply like a woodworm; it is not seen from the outside but it gnaws and rasps.

After my return from imprisonment I was visited by a friend older than myself, mild and intransigent, the cultivator of a personal religion, which, however, always seemed to me severe and serious. He was glad to find me alive and basically unhurt, perhaps matured and fortified, certainly enriched. He told me that my having survived could not be the work of chance, of an accumulation of fortunate circumstances (as I maintained, and still maintain) but rather of Providence. I bore the mark, I was an elect: I, the non-believer, and even less of a believer after the season of Auschwitz, was a person touched by Grace, a saved man. And why just I? It is impossible to know, he answered. Perhaps because I had to write, and by writing bear witness: wasn't I in fact then, in 1946, writing a book about my imprisonment?

Such an opinion seemed monstrous to me. It pained me as when one touches an exposed nerve, and kindled the doubt I spoke of before: I might be alive in the place of another, at the expense of another; I might have usurped, that is, in fact killed. The 'saved' of the Lager were not the best, those predestined to do good; the bearers of a message. What I had seen and lived through proved the exact contrary. Preferably the worst survived, the selfish, the violent, the insensitive, the collaborators of the 'grey zones', the spies. It was not a certain rule (there were none, nor are there certain rules in human matters), but it was, nevertheless, a rule. I felt innocent, yes, but enrolled among the saved and therefore in permanent search of a justification in my own eyes and those of others. The worst survived – that is, the fittest; the best all died.

Chaim died, the watchmaker from Cracow, a pious Jew who despite the language difficulties made an effort to understand and be understood, and explained to me, the foreigner, the essential rules for survival during the first crucial days of captivity; Szabo died, the taciturn Hungarian peasant who was almost two metres tall and so was the hungriest of all, and yet, as long as he had the strength, he did not hesitate to help his weaker companions to pull and push; and Robert, a professor at the Sorbonne who spread courage and trust all around him, spoke five languages, wore himself out recording everything in his prodigious memory, and had he lived would have answered the questions which I do not know how to answer; and Baruch, a docker from Livorno, died immediately, on the first day, because he had answered the first punch he had received with punches and was massacred by three *Kapos* in coalition. These, and innumerable others, died not despite their valour but because of it.

My religious friend had told me that I survived so that I could bear witness. I have done so, as best I could, and I also could not have done so; and I am still doing so, whenever the opportunity presents itself; but the thought that this testifying of mine could by itself gain for me the privilege of surviving and living for many years without serious problems, troubles me, because I cannot see any proportion between the privilege and its outcome.

I must repeat – we, the survivors, are not the true witnesses. This is an uncomfortable notion, of which I have become conscious little by little, reading the memoirs of others and reading mine at a distance of years. We survivors are not only an ex-

iguous but also an anomalous minority: we are those who by
their prevarications or abilities or good luck did not touch
bottom. Those who did so, those who saw the Gorgon, have
not returned to tell about it or have returned mute, but they
are the 'Muslims', the submerged, the complete witnesses, the
ones whose deposition would have a general significance. They
are the rule, we are the exception. Under another sky, and
returned from a similar and diverse slavery, Solzhenitsyn
noted:

> Almost all those who served a long sentence and whom
> you congratulate because they are survivors are unques-
> tionably *pridurki* or were such during the greater part of
> their imprisonment. Because Lagers are meant for ex-
> termination, this should not be forgotten.

In the language of that other concentrationary universe, the
*pridurki* are the prisoners who, in one way or another, conquered a position of privilege, those we called the Prominent.

We who were favoured by fate tried, with more or less
wisdom, to recount not only our fate, but also that of the
others, the submerged; but this was a discourse on 'behalf of
third parties', the story of things seen from close by, not experienced personally. When the destruction was terminated,
the work accomplished was not told by anyone, just as no one
ever returned to recount his own death. Even if they had paper
and pen, the submerged would not have testified because their
death had begun before that of their body. Weeks and months
before being snuffed out, they had already lost the ability to
observe, to remember, compare and express themselves. We
speak in their stead, by proxy.

I could not say whether we did so or do so because of a
kind of moral obligation towards those who were silenced, or
rather in order to free ourselves of their memory; certainly we
do it because of a strong and durable impulse. I do not believe
that psychoanalysts (who have pounced upon our tangles with
professional avidity) are competent to explain this impulse.

Their knowledge was built up and tested 'outside', in the world that, for the sake of simplicity, we call civilian: it traces its phenomenology and tries to explain it; it studies its deviations and tries to heal them. Their interpretations, even those of someone like Bruno Bettelheim who went through the trials of the Lager, seem to me approximate and simplified, as if someone wished to apply the theorems of plain geometry to the solution of spheric triangles. The mental mechanisms of the *Häftlinge* were different from ours; curiously, and in parallel, different also were their physiology and pathology. In the Lager, colds and influenza were unknown, but one died, at times suddenly, from illnesses that the doctors never had an opportunity to study. Gastric ulcers and mental illnesses were healed (or became asymptomatic) but everyone suffered from an unceasing discomfort that polluted sleep and was nameless. To define this as a 'neurosis' is reductive and ridiculous. Perhaps it would be more correct to see in it an atavistic anguish, whose echo one hears in the second verse of *Genesis*: the anguish inscribed in everyone of the 'tohu-bohu' of a deserted and empty universe crushed under the spirit of God, but from which the spirit of man is absent: not yet born or already extinguished.

And there is another, vaster shame, the shame of the world. It was memorably pronounced by John Donne, and quoted innumerable times, pertinently or not, that 'no man is an island', and that every bell tolls for everyone. And yet there are those who faced by the crime of others or their own, turn their backs so as not to see it and not feel touched by it: this is what the majority of Germans did during the twelve Hitlerian years, deluding themselves that not seeing was a way of not knowing, and that not knowing relieved them of their share of complicity or connivance. But we were denied the screen of willed ignorance, T. S. Eliot's 'partial shelter': we were not able not to see. The ocean of pain, past and present, surrounded us, and its level rose from year to year until it almost submerged us. It was useless to close one's eyes or turn one's back to it, because it was all around, in every direction, all the way to the horizon. It was not possible for us, nor did we want, to become islands; the just among us, neither more nor less numerous than in any other human group, felt remorse, shame and pain for the misdeeds that others and not they had committed, and in which they felt involved, because they sensed that what had happened around them in their presence, and in them, was irrevocable. It would never again be able to be cleansed; it would prove that man, the human species – we, in short – were potentially able to construct an infinite enormity of pain; and that pain is the only force that is created from nothing, without cost and without effort. It is enough not to see, not to listen, not to act.

We are often asked, as if our past conferred a prophetic ability upon us, whether Auschwitz will return: whether, that is, other slaughters will take place, unilateral, systematic, mechanised, willed, at a governmental level, perpetrated upon innocent and defenceless populations and legitimised by the doctrine of contempt. Prophets, to our good fortune, we are not, but something can be said. That a similar tragedy, almost ignored in the West, took place in Cambodia around 1975. That the German slaughter could be set off – and after that fed on itself – out of a desire for servitude and smallness of soul, thanks to the concurrence of a number of factors (the state of war; German technological and organisational perfectionism; Hitler's will and inverted charisma; the lack in Germany of solid democratic roots), not very numerous, each of them indispensable but insufficient if taken singly. These factors can occur again and are already recurring in various parts of the world. The convergence again of all of them within ten or twenty years (there is no sense in speaking of a more remote future) is not very likely but also not impossible. In my opinion, a mass slaughter is particularly unlikely in the Western world, Japan, and also the Soviet Union: the Lagers of the Second World War are still part of the memory of many, on both the popular and governmental levels, and a sort of immunisational defence is at work which amply coincides with the shame of which I have spoken.

As to what might happen in other parts of the world, or later on, it is prudent to suspend judgement; and the nuclear apocalypse, certainly bilateral, probably instantaneous and definitive, is a greater and different horror, strange, new, which stands outside the theme I have chosen.

# CHAPTER FOUR

# Communicating

I never liked the term 'incommunicability', so fashionable in the 1970s; first of all because it is a linguistic horror, and in the second place, because of more personal reasons.

In today's normal world, which by convention and contrast we call from time to time 'civilised' or 'free', one almost never encounters a total linguistic barrier: that is, finding oneself facing a human being with whom one must absolutely establish communication or die, and then is unable to do so.

A famous but incomplete example of this was given by Antonioni in his film *Red Desert*, in the episode in which the protagonist meets in the night a Turkish sailor who knows not a word of any language but his own, and tries in vain to make himself understood. Incomplete, because on both sides, also that of the sailor, the will to communicate exists; or at least, the will to reject contact is lacking.

According to a theory fashionable during those years, which to me seems frivolous and irritating, 'incommunicability' supposedly was an unfailing ingredient, a life sentence included in the human condition, and particularly in the way of life of industrial society: we are monads, incapable of reciprocal messages, or capable only of truncated messages, false at their departure, misunderstood on their arrival. Discourse is fictitious, pure noise, a painted veil that conceals existential silence; also, we are alone, even if (or especially if) we live in pairs. It seems to me that this lament originates in mental laziness and points to it; certainly it encourages it, in a dangerous vicious circle. Except for cases of pathological incapacity, one can and must communicate; it is a useful and easy way to contribute to the peace of others and one's own, because silence, the absence of signals, is in its turn a signal, but it is ambiguous, and ambiguity generates anxiety and suspicion. To say that it is impossible to communicate is false; one always can. To refuse to communicate is a failing; we are biologically and socially predisposed to communication, and in particular to its highly evolved and noble form, which is language. All human species speak, no non-human species knows how to speak.

From this communication standpoint – indeed, of failed communication – the experience of us survivors is peculiar. It is an irksome habit of ours to intervene when someone (our children!) speaks about cold, hunger or fatigue. What do you know about it? You should have gone through what we did. In general, for reasons of good taste and good neighbourliness, we try to resist the temptation of such *miles gloriosus* interventions; nevertheless this becomes imperative for me precisely when I hear people talking about failed or impossible communication. 'You should have experienced ours.' It cannot be compared to that of the tourist going to Finland or Japan who finds interlocutors who do not speak his language but are professionally (or even spontaneously) polite or well-intentioned and make an effort to understand and be of help to him. Besides, who, and in what corner of the world, can't string together a few words of English? And the questions of tourists are few, always the same: hence aporias are rare, and almost understanding each other can even be as amusing as a game.

Certainly more dramatic is the case of the Italian immigrant in America a hundred years ago, or the Turk, Moroccan or Pakistani in Germany, or Sweden today. Here we no longer have a brief exploration stripped of the unexpected, conducted down tracks well tested by the travel agencies; it is perhaps a definitive transplanting; an insertion into work which today is rarely elementary, and in which the comprehension of the spoken or written word is necessary; it entails indispensable human relationships with neighbours, clerks, colleagues, and superiors; at work, on the street, at the café, with foreign people whose customs are different, and who are often hostile. But there is no lack of correctives, capitalist society itself is intelligent enough to understand that here its profit coincides with the output of the 'guest worker' and therefore with his well-being and his adjustment. He is granted permission to bring along his family, that is, a piece of his country; for better or worse one finds lodgings for him; he may (often must) attend language school. The deaf mute who got off the train receives help, perhaps without love, not without efficiency, and he soon reacquires speech.

We saw incommunicability in a more radical manner. I refer, in particular, to Italian, Yugoslav and Greek deportees; to a lesser extent to the French, among whom many were of Polish or German extraction, and some, being Alsatian, understood German quite well; and to many Hungarians who came from the countryside. For us Italians, the collision with the linguistic barrier took place dramatically before deportation, still in Italy, at the moment in which the functionaries of the Italian police, with visible reluctance, turned us over to the SS who, in the February of 1944, claimed for itself the management of the processing camp in Fossoli near Modena. We immediately realised, from our very first contacts with the contemptuous men with the black patches, that knowing or not knowing German was a watershed. With those who understood them and answered in an articulate manner, the appearance of a human relationship was established. With those who did not understand them, the black men reacted in a manner that astonished and frightened us: an order that had been pronounced in the calm voice of a man who knows he will be obeyed, was repeated word for word in a loud, angry voice, then screamed at the top of his lungs as if he were addressing a deaf person or indeed a domestic animal, more responsive to the tone than the content of the message.

If anyone hesitated (everyone hesitated, because they did not understand and were terrorised) the blows fell, and it was obvious that they were a variant of the same language: use of the word to communicate thought, this necessary and sufficient mechanism for man to be man, had fallen into disuse. This was a signal. For those people we were no longer men; with us, as with cows or mules, there was no substantial difference between a scream and a punch. For a horse to run or stop, turn, pull or stop pulling, it is not necessary to come to terms with it, or give it detailed explanations; a dictionary made up of a dozen, variously assorted but univocal signs is sufficient. It does not matter whether acoustical, tactile, or visual: pulling on the reins, jabbing the spurs, screams, gestures, cracking the whip, trumpeting with the lips, slams on the back are all equally good. Speaking to it would be a foolish act, just like speaking to oneself, or a ridiculous mawkishness: because what would the horse understand anyway? In his book *Mauthausen* (La Pietra, Milan, 1977), Marsalek tells us that in this Lager, even more polyglot than Auschwitz, the rubber truncheon was called *der Dolmetcher*, the interpreter: the one who made himself understood by everybody.

In fact, an uncultivated man (and Hitler's Germans, and the SS in particular, were frightfully uncultivated; they had not been 'cultivated', or had been badly cultivated) does not know how to distinguish clearly between those who do not understand his language and those who do not understand *tout court*. It had been driven into the young Nazis' heads that in the world there existed only one civilisation, the German; all others, present or past, were acceptable only insofar as they contained some German elements. Thus, whoever did not understand or speak German was a barbarian by definition; if he insisted on expressing himself in his own language, indeed, his non-language, he must be beaten into silence and put back in his place, pulling, carrying and pushing, because he was not a *Mensch*, not a human being.

An eloquent episode returns to my mind. On the work site, the rookie *Kapo* of a squad composed mainly of Italians, Frenchmen and Greeks, had not realised that one of the most feared SS supervisors had approached him fron the back. He turned round abruptly, stood at attention, completely bewildered, and pronounced the prescribed *Meldung* : '83rd

Kommando, forty-two men.' Flustered as he was, he had
actually said '*zwei-und-vierzig Männer*', 'men'. The SS corrected him in a reproachful, paternal tone: that's not what you
say, you say '*zwei-und-vierzig Häftlinge*', forty-two prisoners.
He was a young *Kapo* and therefore forgivable, but he must
learn the trade, the social conventions and hierarchical distances.

This 'not being talked to' had rapid and devastating effects.
To those who do not talk to you, or address you in screams
that seem inarticulate to you, you do not dare speak. If you
are fortunate enough to have next to you someone with whom
you have a language in common, good for you, you'll be able
to exchange your impressions, seek counsel, let off steam,
confide in him; if you don't find anyone, your tongue dries up
in a few days, and your thought with it.

Besides, on the immediate plane, you do not understand
orders and prohibitions, do not decipher instructions, some
futile and absurd, others fundamental. In short you find yourself in a void, and you understand at your expense that
communication generates information and that without information you cannot live. The greater part of the prisoners
who did not understand German – that is, almost all the
Italians – died during the first ten to fifteen days after their
arrival: at first sight, from hunger, cold, fatigue, and disease;
but after a more attentive examination, due to insufficient
information. If they had been able to communicate with their
more experienced companions, they would have been able to
orient themselves better: learn first of all to procure for themselves clothing, shoes, illegal food; avoid the harsher labour
and the often lethal encounters with the SS; handle the inevit-
able illnesses without making fatal mistakes. I don't mean to
say that they would not have died, but they would have lived
longer and had a greater chance of regaining lost ground.

For all of us survivors, who are not exactly polyglot, the
first days in the Lager have remained impressed in our memory
in the form of an out-of-focus and frenzied film, filled with
dreadful sound and fury devoid of meaning: a hubbub of

persons without names or faces drowned in a continuous, deafening background noise, from which, however, the human word did not surface. A black and white film, with sound but not a talkie.

I have noticed, in myself and others who came back, a curious effect of this void and need for communication. At a distance of forty years we still remember, in a purely acoustic form, words and sentences pronounced around us in languages we did not know and did not learn afterwards: in my case, for example, in Polish or Hungarian. To this day I remember how one pronounced in Polish not my registration number but that of the prisoner who preceded me on the roster of a certain hut: a tangle of sounds that ended harmoniously, like the indecipherable counting jingles of children, in something like 'stergishi steri'. (Today I know that these two words mean 'forty-four'.) As a matter of fact, in that hut the soup dispenser and the greater part of the prisoners were Polish, and Polish was the official language; when you were called, you must be there ready, holding out your bowl in order not to miss your turn and, so as not to be caught by surprise, it was a good idea to jump when the companion with the immediately preceding registration number was called. In fact, that 'stergishi steri' functioned like the bell that conditioned Pavlov's dogs: it stimulated an immediate secretion of saliva.

These foreign voices became engraved on our memories as on an empty, blank magnetic tape; in the same manner, a famished stomach rapidly assimilates even indigestible food. Their meaning did not help us remember them, because for us they had none; and yet, much later, we recited them to people who could understand them, and they did have a meaning, tenuous and banal. They were imprecations, curses, or small everyday, often repeated sentences, such as 'What time is it?' or 'I can't walk,' or 'Leave me alone.' They were fragments torn from the indistinct; the fruit of a useless and unconscious effort to carve a meaning or sense out of the senseless. They were also the mental equivalent of our bodily need for nourishment, which drove us to search for potato peelings around the kitchens: little more than nothing, better than nothing. Also the undernourished brain suffers from a specific hunger of its own. Or perhaps this useless and paradoxical memory had another significance and purpose: it was the unconscious preparation for 'later', for an improbable survival, in which every shred of experience would become a tessera in a vast mosaic.

In the first pages of *The Truce*, I described an extreme case of necessary and failed communication: that of the three-year-old child Hurbinek, perhaps born clandestinely in the Lager, whom nobody had taught to speak and who had an intense need to speak, expressed by its entire poor body. Even from this point of view, the Lager was a cruel laboratory in which one could witness situations and behaviours never seen before nor after nor anywhere else.

A few years earlier I had learned some German words, when I was still a student, for the sole purpose of understanding textbooks of chemistry and physics: certainly not to actively transmit my thought or understand the spoken language. Those were the years of the Fascist racial laws, and my meeting a German, or taking a trip to Germany, seemed quite improbable events. Flung into Auschwitz, despite my initial bewilderment (actually, perhaps indeed thanks to it) I soon understood that my extremely meagre *Wortschatz* had become an essential factor of survival. *Wortschatz* means 'lexical patrimony', but, literally, 'treasure of words'; never was a term more appropriate. Knowing German meant life: I only had to look around me. My Italian companions did not understand it. Almost all, with the exception of a few from Trieste, were drowning one by one in the stormy sea of not-understanding: they did not know what the orders meant, they received slaps and kicks without comprehending why. The camp's rudimentary ethic stipulated that a blow must in some way be justified, so as to facilitate the establishment of the trans-gression–punishment–repentance parabola; therefore the *Kapo* or his substitutes often accompanied the blow with a grunt:

'You know why?' which was followed by a summary 'communication of the crime'. But for the new deaf and dumb this ceremonial was useless. They instinctively sought refuge in corners to protect their backs; aggression could come from all directions. They looked around them with bewildered eyes, like trapped animals, and that is what they had actually become.

For many Italians, the help of French and Spanish companions whose languages were less 'foreign' than German was vital. In Auschwitz there were no Spaniards while the French (more precisely, the deportees from France or Belgium) were many, perhaps ten per cent of the total in 1944. Some were Alsatians, or German or Polish Jews who during the preceding decade had sought a refuge in France that turned out to be a trap: all of these knew German or Yiddish well or badly. The other, metropolitan French, proletarians or bourgeois or intellectuals had one or two years earlier been subjected to a selection analogous to ours: those who did not understand had disappeared from the scene. Those who remained, almost all *métèques*, in the past received rather grudgingly in France, had taken a sad *revanche*. They were our natural interpreters: they translated for us the fundamental commands and warnings of the day, 'Get up', 'Assembly', 'Line up for bread', 'Who's got broken shoes?', 'By threes', 'By fives', et cetera.

Certainly this was not enough. I implored one of them, an Alsatian, to give me a private and accelerated course, spread over brief lessons administered in a whisper, between the moment of curfew and the moment when we gave way to sleep; lessons to be recompensed with bread, since there was no other currency. He accepted, and I believe that never was bread better spent. He explained to me what the roars of the *Kapos* and SS meant, the foolish or ironic mottoes written in Gothic letters on the hut's roof trusses, what was the meaning of the colours of the triangles we wore on our chests above the registration number. So I realised that the German of the Lager – skeletal, howled, studded with obscenities and imprecations – was only vaguely related to the precise, austere language of my chemistry books, and to the melodious, refined German of Heine's poetry that Clara, a classmate of mine, would recite to me.

I did not realise, and I realised this only much later, that the Lager's German was a language apart: to say it precisely in German, it was *Orts- und zeitgebunden*, tied to the place and time. It was a variant, particularly barbarised, of what a German Jewish philologist, Klemperer, had called *Lingua Tertii Imperii*, the language of the Third Reich, actually proposing for it the acronym LTI with an ironic analogy to the hundred others (NSDAP, SS, SA, SD, KZ, RKPA, WVHA, RSHA, BDM . . .) dear to the Germany of that time.

About LTI, and its Italian equivalent, much has already been written, also by linguists. It is an obvious observation that where violence is inflicted on man, it is also inflicted on language; and in Italy we have not forgotten the foolish Fascist campaigns against the dialects, against 'barbarisms', against the Valdostan, Valsusan, and Altoatesin place names, against the '*lei* form of address, servile and foreign'. In Germany things were otherwise: for centuries the German language had shown a spontaneous aversion from words of non-German origin, so that German scientists had rushed to rename bronchitis as 'air-pipes-inflammation', the duodenum as 'twelve-finger-intestine', and pyrruvic acid as 'burn-grapes-acid'; therefore, from this point of view, Nazism, which wanted to purify everything, had very little left to purify. LTI differed from Goethe's German chiefly because of certain semantic shifts, and the abuse of certain terms: for example, the adjective *volkisch* ('national folk') had become omnipresent and laden with nationalistic arrogance and the connotation of the adjective *fanatisch* had changed from negative to positive.

But in the archipelago of German Lagers there had taken shape a sectorial language, a jargon, the 'Lager jargon', subdivided into specific sub-jargons peculiar to each Lager and closely related to the old German of Prussian barracks and the new German of the SS. It is not surprising that it proves to run parallel to the jargon of Soviet labour camps, several terms of which are cited by Solzhenitsyn; every one of these has an exact counterpart in Lager jargon. The translation into German of *The Gulag Archipelago* cannot have presented many difficulties; or if it did, not those of terminology.

Common to all Lagers was the term *Muselmann*, 'Muslim', given to the irreversibly exhausted, worn-out prisoner close to death. Two explanations for it have been advanced, neither very convincing: fatalism, and the head bandages that could resemble a turban. It is mirrored exactly, even in its cynical irony, by the Russian term *dokodjaga*, literally 'come to an end', 'concluded'. In the Ravensbrück Lager (the only one exclusively for women) the same concept was expressed, so I'm told by Lydia Rolfi, by the two specular substantives *Schmutzstück* and *Schmuckstück*, which were, respectively, 'garbage' and 'jewel', almost homophonous, one the parody of the other. The Italian women did not understand their chilling significance, and unified the two terms in one pronouncing it 'smistig'. 'Prominent' is also a term common to all the sub-jargons. Concerning the 'Prominent', the prisoners who had come up in the world, I've spoken at length in *If This Is A Man*; being an indispensable component of camp sociology they existed also in the Soviet camps, where (I mentioned this in the third chapter) they were called *pridurki*.

In Auschwitz, 'to eat' was rendered with *fressen*, a verb which in good German is applied only to animals. For 'go away' the expression *hau'ab* was used, the imperative mode of the verb *abhauen*; this, in proper German, means 'to cut, chop off', but in Lager jargon it was equivalent to 'go to hell, get out of the way'. It once happened to me that I used this expression (*Jetzt hauen wir ab*) in good faith shortly after the end of the war to take leave of certain well-mannered functionaries of the Bayer Company after a business meeting. It was as if I had said, 'Now let's get the hell out of here.' They looked at me with astonishment: the term belonged to a linguistic register different from that in which our preceding conversation had been conducted and is certainly not taught in foreign-language courses. I explained to them that I had not learned

German in school but rather in a Lager called Auschwitz; this gave rise to a certain embarrassment, but since I was in the role of buyer they continued to treat me with courtesy. I also realised later on that my pronunciation is coarse, but I deliberately did not try to make it more genteel; for the same reason, I have never had the tattoo removed from my left arm.

Lager jargon, as is only natural, was strongly influenced by other languages spoken in the Lager and its surroundings: by Polish, Yiddish, Salesian dialect, later on by Hungarian. From the background racket of my first days of imprisonment there immediately emerged, with insistence, four or five expressions that were not German; they must, I thought, indicate some basic object or activity, such as work, water, and bread. They became engraved in my memory, in the curious mechanical manner I described before. Only much later a Polish friend unwillingly explained to me that they simply meant 'cholera', 'blood of a dog', 'thunder', 'son of a whore', and 'screwed'; the first three having the function of exclamations.

Yiddish was *de facto* the camp's second language (replaced later on by Hungarian). Not only did I not understand it, I only vaguely knew about its existence, based on some quotation or joke heard from my father who had worked for a few years in Hungary. The Polish, Russian and Hungarian Jews were astonished that we Italians did not speak it: we were suspect Jews, not to be trusted; besides being, naturally, 'Badoglios' for the SS and 'Mussolinis' for the French, the Greeks and the political prisoners. Also, leaving aside the problems of communication, it was not comfortable to be Italian Jews. As is by now well known after the deserved success of the books of the Singer brothers and others, Yiddish is substantially an ancient German dialect, different from modern German both in lexicon and pronunciation. It caused me greater anguish than Polish, which I did not understand at all, because I should have understood it. I listened to it with strained attentiveness: often it was difficult for me to understand whether a sentence addressed to me or spoken near me was German or Yiddish or a hybrid. In fact, some well-intentioned Polish Jews made an effort to Germanise their Yiddish as much as they could so I could understand them.

Of the Yiddish breathed in with the air, I found a singular trace in *If This Is A Man*. In the chapter entitled 'Kraus', a dialogue is reported: Gounan, a French Jew of Polish extraction, addresses the Hungarian Kraus with the sentence *'Langsam, du blöder Einer, langsam, verstanden?'* which translated word by word is 'Slow, you stupid one, slow, understood?' It did sound a bit strange, but I really thought I had heard it like that (these were recent memories; I was writing in 1946), and I transcribed it just like that. My German translator was very doubtful: I must have heard or remembered incorrectly. After a long epistolary discussion, he suggested that the expression be altered, that it did not appear acceptable to him. In fact, in the translation that was then published it goes like this: *'Langsam, du blöder Heini . . .'* where Heini is the diminutive of Heinrich, Henry. But recently, in a fine book about the history and structure of Yiddish, *Mama Loshen* by J. Geipel, I found that the form *'Khamoyer du einer!'* – 'Dunce you one!' – is typical of the language. Mechanical memory had functioned correctly.

Not all suffered to the same extent because of failed or limited communication. Not to suffer from it, to accept the eclipse of the word was an ominous symptom: it signalled the approach of definitive indifference. A few, solitary by nature, or already habituated to isolation in their 'civilian' life, gave no sign of suffering from it; but the greater part of the prisoners who had overcome the critical phase of initiation tried to protect themselves, each in his own way; some begging for shreds of information, some spreading without discernment triumphant or disastrous information, true, false, or invented, some who sharpened eyes and ears to seize and try to interpret all signs offered by men, the earth and the heavens. But to the limited internal communication was added the limited communication with the external world. In several Lagers, isolation was total; mine, Monowitz-Auschwitz, could from this standpoint be considered privileged. Almost every week there arrived 'new' prisoners from all the countries of occupied Europe, who brought with them recent news, often as eyewitnesses; in spite of prohibitions and the danger of being denounced to the Gestapo, in the huge work site we spoke with Polish and German workers, at times even with English prisoners-of-war; in the garbage cans we found newspapers which were a few days old and read them avidly. An enterprising work companion of mine, bilingual because he was Alsatian and a journalist by profession, even boasted of having taken out a subscription for the *Völkischer Beobachter*, the most authoritative daily German newspaper of the time: what could be easier? He had begged a trustworthy German worker to subscribe and had taken over the subscription by giving him a gold tooth. Every morning, during the long wait of the roll-call, he gathered us together and gave us an accurate summary of the day's news.

On 7 June 1944 we saw the English prisoners on their way to work, and there was something different about them: they marched well aligned, chests thrust forward, smiling, martial, with a step so eager that the German sentinel who escorted them, a territorial no longer young, had difficulty keeping up with them. They saluted us with the V-sign of victory. The next day we found out that from a clandestine radio of theirs they had learned about the Allied landings in Normandy, and that was a great day for us too: freedom seemed within reach. But in most camps things were much worse. The newcomers arrived from other Lagers or ghettos which in turn were cut off from the world and so brought with them only the horrendous local news. Work did not, as with us, take place in contact with free workers from ten or twelve different countries, but on farms, small workshops, stone or sand quarries, even mines: and in the mine-Lagers, conditions were the same as led to the death of the war-slaves of the Romans and the Indios subjugated by the Spanish; so lethal that no one returned to describe them. As said before, the news 'from the world' that reached us was sporadic and vague. We felt forgotten, like the condemned who were left to die in medieval *oubliettes*.

The Jews, enemies by definition, impure and sowers of impurity, destroyers of the world, were forbidden that most precious communication, contact with their country of origin and their family. Whoever has experienced exile, in any of its many forms, knows how much one suffers when this nerve is severed. This leads to a deadly impression of desertion, and also to unjust resentment: why won't they write to me? why don't they help me, they who are free? We were able to understand very well, then, that in the great continent of freedom, freedom of communication is an important province. As is the case with health, only the person who loses it realises its true value. But one does not suffer from it only on an individual level. In countries and epochs in which communication is impeded, all other liberties soon wither; discussion dies by inanition, ignorance of the opinion of others becomes rampant, imposed opinions triumph; the well-known example of this is the crazy genetics preached in the USSR by Lysenko, which in the absence of discussions (his opponents were exiled to Siberia) compromised the harvests for twenty years. Intolerance is inclined to censor, and censorship increases the ignorance of the arguments of others and thus intolerance itself: a rigid vicious circle that is hard to break.

The weekly hour when our 'political' companions received mail from home was for us the saddest, when we felt the whole burden of being different, estranged, cut off from our country, indeed from the human race. It was the hour when we felt the tattoo burn like a wound, and the certainty that none of us would return overwhelmed us like an avalanche of mud. In any case, even if we had been allowed to write a letter – to whom would we have addressed it? The families of the Jews of Europe were submerged or dispersed or destroyed.

I was given the rare good fortune (I told about it in *Moments of Reprieve*) of being able to exchange some letters with my family. For this I am indebted to two persons very different from each other: an old, almost illiterate bricklayer and a courageous young woman, Bianca Guidetta Serra, who is now a well-known attorney. I know that this was one of the factors that allowed me to survive: but, as I said before, each of us survivors is in more than one way an exception; something that we ourselves, to exorcise the past, tend to forget.

# CHAPTER FIVE

# Useless Violence

The title of this chapter may seem provocative or even offensive. Is there such a thing as useful violence? Unfortunately, yes. Death, even when not provoked, even the most clement, is a violence, but it is sadly useful: a world of immortals (Swift's Strulbruggs) would be neither conceivable nor liveable, would be more violent than the present life, violent though it is. Nor, in general, is murder useless: Raskolnikov, in killing the old moneylender, set a purpose for himself, even though it was a culpable one; and so Princip at Sarajevo and Aldo Moro's kidnappers in Via Fani. Leaving aside the cases of homicidal madness, anyone who kills knows why he does so: for money, to eliminate a true or presumed enemy, or to avenge an insult. Wars are detestable; they are a very bad way to settle controversies between nations or factions, but they cannot be called useless: they aim at a goal, though it may be wicked or perverse. They are not gratuitous, their purpose is not to inflict suffering; suffering is there, it is collective, anguishing, unjust, but it is a by-product, something extra. Now, I believe that the twelve Hitlerian years shared their violence with many other historical space-times, but that they were characterised by widespread useless violence, as an end in itself, with the sole purpose of creating pain, occasionally having a purpose, yet always redundant, always disproportionate to the purpose itself.

Thinking back with the wisdom of hindsight to those years that devastated Europe and in the end Germany itself, one feels torn between two opinions. Were we witnessing the rational development of an inhuman plan or a manifestation (until now unique in history and still unsatisfactorily explained) of collective madness? Logic intent on evil, or the absence of logic? As so often in human affairs, the two alternatives coexisted. There is no doubt that the fundamental design of National Socialism had a rationality of its own: the drive towards the East (an old German dream), the stifling of the workers' movements, hegemony over continental Europe, annihilation of Bolshevism and Judaism which Hitler simplistically identified with one another, the sharing of world power with England and the United States, the apotheosis of the Germanic race with the 'Spartan' elimination of the mentally ill and useless mouths: all these elements were compatible with one another and can be deduced from a few postulates already presented with undeniable clarity in *Mein Kampf*: arrogance and radicalism, hubris and *Gründlichkeit* (thoroughness); insolent logic, not insanity.

Hateful also, but not insane, were the means foreseen to achieve these ends: to unleash military aggressions or ruthless wars, support internal Fifth Columns, transfer or remove entire populations, subjugate them, sterilize them, or exterminate them. Neither Nietzsche nor Hitler nor Rosenberg were mad when they intoxicated themselves and their followers by preaching the myth of the Superman, to whom everything is permitted in recognition of his dogmatic and congenital superiority; but worthy of meditation is the fact that all of them, teacher and pupils, became progressively removed from reality as little by little their morality came unglued from the morality common to all times and all civilisations, which is an integral part of our human heritage and which in the end must be acknowledged.

Rationality ceases, and the disciples have amply surpassed (and betrayed!) the teacher, precisely in the practice of useless cruelty. Nietzsche's message is profoundly repugnant to me; I find it difficult to discover an affirmation in it which is not contrary to what I like to think; his oracular tone irritates me; yet it seems to me that a desire for the sufferings of others cannot be found in it. Indifference, yes, almost on every page, but never *Schadenfreude*, the joy in your neighbour's misfortune, and even less the joy of deliberately inflicting suffering. The pain of *hoi polloi*, of the *Ungestalten*, the shapeless, the not-born-noble, is a price that must be paid for the advent of the reign of the elect; it is a minor evil, but still an evil; it is not in itself desirable. Hitlerian doctrine and practice were much different.

Many of the useless Nazi violences by now belong to history: it is enough to think of the 'disproportionate' massacres of the Ardeatine Caves, of Oradour, Lidice, Boves, Marzabotto and too many more, in which the limits of reprisal, already intrinsically inhuman, were enormously surpassed; but other minor, individual violences remain inscribed with indelible letters in the memory of each of us ex-deportees, details of the larger picture.

Almost always, at the beginning of the memory sequence, stands the train which marked the departure towards the unknown not only for chronological reasons but also for the gratuitous cruelty with which those (otherwise innocuous) convoys of ordinary freight cars were employed for an extraordinary purpose.

There is not a diary or story, among our many such accounts, in which the train does not appear, the sealed boxcar changed from a commercial vehicle into an ambulatory prison or even an instrument of death. It is always packed, but the number of persons who, on each occasion, were jammed into it seems to be based on a rough calculation: from fifty to one hundred and twenty, depending on the length of the journey and the hierarchic level that the Nazi system assigned to the 'human material' being transported.

The convoys leaving Italy contained 'only' fifty to sixty persons per car (Jews, politicals, Partisans, unfortunates who had been rounded up on the streets, military personnel captured after the débâcle of 8 September 1943): it may be that distances were taken into account or perhaps even the impression that these trains would make on possible witnesses present along the route. At the opposite extreme stood the transports of Eastern Europe: Slavs, especially if Jewish, were lesser merchandise, almost totally devoid of value indeed; they would in any case die, no matter whether during the journey or afterwards. The convoys that transported Polish Jews from ghettos to Lagers, or from Lager to Lager, contained up to a hundred and twenty persons per car: their journey was brief . . .

Now, fifty persons in a freight car are most uncomfortable; they can all lie down simultaneously to rest, but body against body. If they are one hundred or more, even a trip of a few hours is an inferno. One must take turns standing or squatting, and often, among the travellers, there are old people, sick people, children, nursing women, lunatics, or individuals who go mad during the journey and because of the journey.

In the procedure of Nazi railway transports, variables and constants can be distinguished. It is not possible for us to know whether this procedure was based on a regulation or whether the functionaries in charge had a free hand. Constant was the hypocritical advice (or order) to bring along as much as possible: especially gold, jewels, valuable currency, furs, in certain cases (certain transports of Jewish farmers from Hungary and Slovakia) even small livestock. 'It's all stuff that will come in handy,' the escort personnel said out of the side of their mouths and with an air of complicity. In fact, this was self-plunder; it was a simple and ingenious ruse to bring valuables into the Reich, without publicity, bureaucratic complications, special transports, or fear of thefts en route: and sure enough, at the arrival, everything was seized. Constant was the total bareness of the cars. The German authorities, for a journey that might last as long as two weeks (as was the case with Jews deported from Salonika) literally did not provide anything; neither foodstuffs, nor water, nor mats, nor straw to cover the wooden floor, nor receptacles for bodily needs, and neither did they bother to alert the local authorities or the directors of the collection camps (when they existed), to provide these in some way or other. A notice would not have cost nothing: but, precisely, this systematic negligence became a useless cruelty, a deliberate creation of pain which was an end in itself.

In some cases the prisoners destined for deportation were able to learn something from experience. They had seen other convoys leave and learned at the expense of their predecessors that they themselves must take care of all these logistical necessities, as best they could, and conform with the limitations imposed by the Germans.

Typical is the case of the trains that left from the collection camp of Westerbork in the Netherlands. This was an enormous camp, with tens of thousands of Jewish prisoners, and Berlin expected the local commander to send off every week a train with approximately one thousand deportees: altogether, ninety-three trains left Westerbork headed for Auschwitz, Sobibor and other minor camps. The survivors were approximately five hundred and none of them travelled in the first convoys whose occupants had departed blindly, with the unfounded hope that the more elementary needs for a three-to-four-day journey would be administratively supplied; as a result, we don't know how many there were who died in transit, nor how the terrifying journey unfolded, because no one returned to tell about it. But after a few weeks a worker at the Westerbork infirmary, a perspicacious observer, noticed that the boxcars of the convoys were always the same: they shuttled between the Lager of departure and that of destination. So it happened that some among those who were deported after that were able to send messages hidden in the cars that returned empty, and from then on it was possible to provide at least some foodstuffs and water, and a barrel for excrement.

The convoy on which I was deported in February 1944 was the first to leave from the Fossoli collection camp (others had left earlier from Rome and Milan, but we had not heard about them). The SS who shortly before had ousted the Italian police from the camp management gave no precise instructions for the journey; they only made it known that it would be long and they let trickle through the interested and ironic advice that I have mentioned already – 'bring along gold and jewels,

and above all woollen clothing and furs, because you're going
to work in a cold country.' The head of the camp, also a
deportee, had the good sense to procure a reasonable supply of
food, but not of water: water doesn't cost anything, isn't that
so? And the Germans don't give anything away, but they are
good organisers ... Neither did he think of equipping each
boxcar with a receptacle that would serve as a latrine, and this
oversight proved to be most serious: it gave rise to a much
worse affliction than thirst and cold.

In my car there were quite a few old people, men and
women: among others, there were all the inmates of the Jewish
Rest Home of Venice. For everybody, but especially for them,
evacuating in public was painful or even impossible: a trauma
for which civilisation does not prepare us, a deep wound inflicted on human dignity, an aggression which is obscene and
ominous; but also the sign of deliberate and gratuitous viciousness. It was our paradoxical luck (but I hesitate to write
this word in this context) that in our car there were also two
young mothers with their infants of a few months and one of
them had brought along a chamber pot: one only, and it had
to serve about fifty people. Two days into the journey we found
some nails stuck into the wooden sides. We pushed two of
them into a corner and with a piece of string and a blanket we
improvised a screen, which was substantially symbolic: we are
not yet animals, we will not be animals as long as we try to
resist.

What happened in the other cars, which did not have this
minimal equipment, is difficult to imagine. The convoy was
stopped two or three times in the open countryside, the doors
of the freight cars were opened and the prisoners were allowed
to get off; but not to walk away from the tracks nor go off on
their own. The doors were opened another time, but during a
stop in an Austrian railroad station. The SS escort did not hide
their amusement at the sight of men and women squatting
wherever they could, on the platforms and in the middle of the
tracks, and the German passengers openly expressed their
disgust: people like this deserve their fate, just look how they

behave. These are not *Menschen*, human beings, but animals, it's clear as the light of day.

This was actually a prologue. In the life that was to follow, the daily rhythm of the Lager, the offence to modesty represented, at least at the beginning, an important part of the global suffering. It was neither easy nor painless to get used to the enormous collective latrine, at brief and obligatory times, in the presence, right in front of you, of the candidate to the succession; on his feet, impatient, at times pleading, at others bullying, every ten seconds he insists: '*Hast du gemacht?*' 'Aren't you finished yet?'

Nevertheless, within a few weeks, the discomfort became attenuated, and then vanished. In its place came (not for everyone) habituation, which is a charitable way of saying that the transformation from human beings into animals was well on its way. I do not believe that this transformation was ever planned or formulated in so many words at any level of the Nazi hierarchy, in any document, any 'labour meeting'. It was a logical consequence of the system: an inhuman regime spreads and extends its inhumanity in all directions, also and especially downwards. Unless it meets with resistance and exceptionally strong characters, it corrupts both its victims and its opponents. The useless cruelty of violated modesty conditioned the existence of all Lagers. The women of Birkenau tell how once, having acquired a precious receptacle (a large bowl of enamelled metal), they had to employ it for three distinct uses: draw their soup; evacuate into it at night when access to the latrines was forbidden; and wash themselves when there was water at the troughs. In all the camps, the rations included a litre of soup a day; in our Lager by concession of the chemical plant for which we worked we got two litres. So there was a lot of water to be evacuated and this forced us to ask permission to go to the latrines frequently or to manage otherwise in the corners of the work site. Some of the prisoners were unable to control themselves. Due to bladder weakness, attacks of fear, neurosis, they were overcome by an urgent need to urinate and often wet themselves, and for this they were punished and derided. An Italian of my age, sleeping in the third tier of the bunk beds, had an accident one night and wet the occupants of the tier below, who immediately reported the event to the *Kapo* of the hut. He swooped down on the Italian who, against all evidence, denied the charge. At that the *Kapo* ordered him to urinate there and then, to prove his innocence; naturally he did not succeed and was given a severe beating, but despite his reasonable request he was not transferred to a lower berth. This was an administrative act, which would have entailed too many complications for the hut's scribe.

Similar to the excremental coercion was the coercion of nudity. One entered the Lager naked: indeed more than naked, deprived not only of clothing and shoes (which were confiscated) but of the hair of one's head and all other hairs. The same is or was done on entry into the military barracks, no doubt, but here the shaving was total and weekly; public and collective nudity was a recurrent condition, typical and laden with significance. This too was a violence with some roots in necessity (it is clear that one must undress for a shower or a medical examination), but offensive because of its useless redundancy. The day in the Lager was studded with innumerable harsh strippings: checking for lice, searching one's clothes, examining for scabies and for the morning wash-up; and also for the periodic selections during which a 'commission' decided who was still fit for work and who, on the contrary, was marked for elimination. Now a naked and barefoot man feels that all his nerves and tendons are severed: he is a helpless prey. Clothes, even the foul clothes which were distributed, even the crude clogs with their wooden soles, are a tenuous but indispensable defence. Anyone who does not have them no longer perceives himself as a human being, but rather as a worm: naked, slow, ignoble, prone on the ground. He knows that he can be crushed at any moment.

The same debilitating sensation of impotence and destitution was produced during the first days of imprisonment by the lack of a spoon: this is a detail that may appear marginal to those who since childhood are used to the abundance of tools at the disposal of even the poorest of kitchens, but it was not marginal. Without a spoon, the daily soup could not be consumed in any other way than by lapping it up as dogs do. Only after many days of apprenticeship (and here, too, how important it was to be immediately able to understand and make oneself understood!) one discovered that there were spoons in the camp but that one had to buy them on the black market with soup or bread: usually a spoon cost half a bread ration or a litre of soup, but inexperienced newcomers were always asked for much more. And yet, when the camp at Auschwitz was liberated, we found in the warehouse thousands of brand-new transparent plastic spoons, besides tens of thousands of spoons made of aluminium, steel or even silver that came from the luggage of deportees as they arrived. So it was not a matter of thrift, but a precise intent to humiliate. The episode narrated in *Judges* 7.5 comes back to mind, in which the warrior Gideon chooses the best among his warriors by observing how they behave while drinking at the river: he rejects all those who lap up the water 'as does the dog' or kneel, and accepts only those who drink standing up, lifting their hands to their mouths.

I would hesitate to define as totally useless other harassments and violences that have been repeatedly and consistently described by all the Lager memorialists. It is well known that in all camps, once or twice a day, a roll-call took place. It certainly was not a nominal roll-call which with thousands or tens of thousands of prisoners would have been impossible: all the more so because they were never referred to by name but only by the five or six digits on the registration number. It was *Zählappell*, a complicated and laborious counting-call which had to take into consideration prisoners transferred to other camps or to the infirmary the evening before and those who had died during the night because the present number must square exactly with the figures of the preceding day. The counting by fives took place as the squads heading for work filed by. Eugen Kogan reports that in Buchenwald the dead and dying also had to show up for the evening roll-call; stretched out on the ground rather than on their feet, they too had to be aligned by fives, to facilitate the count.

This roll-call took place (in the open, naturally) in any weather and lasted at least an hour, or two or three if the count did not balance out; and even twenty-four hours or longer if an escape was suspected. When it rained or snowed, or the cold was intense, it became a torture, even worse than the labour to whose fatigue it was added in the evening. It was perceived as an empty and ritual ceremony, but it probably was not. It was not useless, as in any case, when seen from this angle, neither hunger nor exhausting labour were useless, and not even (may I be forgiven the cynicism: I am trying to reason with a logic that isn't mine) the death by gas of adults and children. All these sufferings were the development of a theme, that of the presumed right of a superior people to subjugate or eliminate an inferior people; such was also that roll-call, which in our dreams of 'afterwards' had become the very emblem of the Lager, summing up in itself the fatigue, cold, hunger and frustration. The suffering it caused, and which in the winter led every day to some breakdowns or deaths, fits into the system, the tradition of the drill (English in origin); the ferocious military practice which was a Prussian inheritance and which Buchner had immortalised in *Wozzeck*.

Besides, it seems evident to me that in many of its painful and absurd aspects the concentrationary world was only a version, an adaptation of German military procedures. The army of prisoners in the Lagers had to be an inglorious copy of the army proper: or, more accurately, its caricature. An army has a uniform: the soldier's uniform is clean, honoured, and covered with insignia, while that of the *Häftling* is filthy, dull and grey; but both had five buttons, or else there's trouble. An army marches by with a military step, in close order, to the sound of a band: so there must be a band also in the Lager, and the march past must be a march past by the book, with 'eyes left' before the reviewing stand and to the sound of music. This ceremony is so necessary, so obvious, as even to prevail over the anti-Jewish legislation of the Third Reich: with paranoid sophistry, this legislation prohibited Jewish orchestras and musicians from playing the scores of Aryan composers because the scores would be contaminated by it. But in the Lagers filled with Jews there were no Aryan musicians, nor, for that matter, are there many military marches written by Jewish composers; therefore, waiving the rules of purity, Auschwitz was the only German place where Jewish musicians could, indeed must, play Aryan music. Necessity knows no rules.

A barracks heritage also was the ritual of 'making the beds'. Of course, this locution is largely euphemistic; where there were bunk beds, each berth was composed of a thin mattress filled with wood shavings, two blankets and a straw pillow, and as a rule two people slept on it. The beds had to be made immediately after reveille, simultaneously throughout the hut. It was therefore necessary for the occupants of the lower bunks to manage as best they could to fix mattress and blanket between the legs of the tenants of the upper levels, who were in precarious balance on the wooden rims and were also intent on the same job. All beds had to be put in order within a minute or two, because the bread distribution began immediately after. Those were frantic moments: the atmosphere filled with nervous tension, with dust to the point of becoming opaque, and curses were exchanged in all languages, because 'making beds' (*Bettenbauen*: this was the technical term) was a sacral operation to be performed in accordance with iron rules. The mattress, fetid with mould and strewn with suspect stains, had to be fluffed up. For that purpose there existed two slits in the lining, through which one could insert the hands. One of the two blankets was supposed to be turned under the mattress, and the other spread out over the pillow in such a way as to form a neat step, with sharp edges. When the operation was finished, the ensemble must look like a rectangular parallelepiped with well smoothed edges, on which was placed the smaller parallelepiped of the pillow.

For the SS in the camp, and consequently for all barracks

heads, *Bettenbauen* had a prime and indecipherable importance: perhaps it was a symbol of order and discipline. Anyone who did not make his bed properly, or forgot to make it, was punished publicly and savagely; furthermore, in every barracks there existed a pair of functionaries, the *Bettnachzieher* ('bed after-pullers': a term that I do not believe exists in normal German and that Goethe certainly would not have understood) whose task it was to check every single bed and then take care of its transversal alignment. For this purpose, they were equipped with a string the length of the hut: they stretched it over the made-up beds, and rectified down to the centimetre any possible deviations. Rather than a cause of torment, this maniacal order seemed absurd and grotesque. In fact, the mattress levelled out with so much care had no consistency whatever, and in the evening, under the weight of the bodies, it immediately flattened down to the slats that supported it. As a matter of fact, one slept on wood.

Within much more extended limits, one gains the impression that throughout all of Hitlerian Germany the barracks code and etiquette replaced those which were traditional and 'bourgeois': the insipid violence of the drill had already in 1934 begun to invade the field of education and was turned against the German people themselves. Those newspapers of the period which had preserved a certain freedom in reporting and criticism tell us about exhausting marches imposed on adolescent boys and girls within the framework of premilitary exercises: up to fifty kilometres a day, with knapsacks on their shoulders and no pity for stragglers. Parents and doctors who dared to protest were threatened with political sanctions.

Altogether different is what must be said about the tattoo, an autochthonous Auschwitzian invention. From the beginning in 1942 in Auschwitz and the Lagers under its jurisdiction (by 1944 they were about forty) the prisoner's registration number was no longer sewed only to his clothes but tattooed on his left forearm. Only non-Jewish German prisoners were exempt from this rule. The operation was performed with methodical rapidity by specialised 'scribes' at the moment of the new arrival's registration, whether coming from freedom, other camps, or the ghettos. In deference to the typically German talent for classification, a true and proper code soon began to take shape: men must be tattooed on the outside of the arm and women on the inside; the numbers of the *Zigeuner*, the gypsies, must be preceded by a Z. The numbers of the Jews, starting in May 1944 (that is, with the mass arrival of Hungarian Jews) must be preceded by an A, which shortly after was replaced by a B. Until September 1944 there were no children in Auschwitz, they were all killed by gas on arrival. After this date, there began to arrive entire families of Poles arrested at random during the Warsaw insurrection: all of them were tattooed, including new-born babies.

The operation was not very painful and lasted no more than a minute, but it was traumatic. Its symbolic meaning was clear to everyone: this is an indelible mark, you will never leave here; this is the mark with which slaves are branded and cattle sent to the slaughter, and that is what you have become. You no longer have a name; this is your new name. The violence of the tattoo was gratuitous, an end in itself, pure offence. Were the three canvas numbers sewed to pants, jackets and winter coat not enough? No, they were not enough: something more was needed, a non-verbal message, so that the innocent would feel his sentence written on his flesh. It was also a return to barbarism, all the more perturbing for orthodox Jews: in fact, precisely in order to distinguish Jews from the barbarians, the tattoo is forbidden by Mosaic law (*Leviticus* 19.28).

At a distance of forty years, my tattoo has become a part of my body. I don't glory in it, nor am I ashamed of it, I do not display and do not hide it. I show it unwillingly to those who ask out of pure curiosity; readily, and with anger, to those who say they are incredulous. Often young people ask me why I don't have it erased, and this surprises me: why should I? There are not many of us in the world to bear this witness.

It is necessary to do (useful?) violence to oneself, to induce

oneself to speak of the fate of the most helpless. I try once
again to follow a logic that isn't mine. For an orthodox Nazi it
must have been obvious, definitive, clear that all Jews must be
killed: that was a dogma, a postulate. The children also, of
course and especially pregnant women, so that no future
enemies should be born. But why, during the furious round-
ups in all the cities and villages of their boundless empire,
violate the houses of the dying? Why go to the trouble of
dragging them on to their trains, take them to die far away,
after a senseless journey, die in Poland on the threshold of the
gas chambers? In my convoy there were two dying ninety-
year-old women, taken out of the Fossoli infirmary: one of
them died en route, nursed in vain by her daughters. Would it
not have been simpler, more 'economical', to let them die, or
perhaps kill them in their beds, instead of adding their agony
to the collective agony of the transport? One is truly led to
think that, in the Third Reich, the best choice, the choice
imposed from above, was the one that entailed the greatest
amount of affliction, the greatest amount of waste, of physical
and moral suffering. The 'enemy' must not only die, but must
die in torment.

Much has been written about work in the Lagers; I myself
have described it in the past. Work was not paid; that is, it
was slave work, one of the three purposes of the concentrationary system. The other two were the elimination of political
adversaries and the extermination of the so-called inferior
races. Let it be said in passing: the Soviet concentrationary
regime differed from the Nazi regime essentially because of the
absence of the third term and the prevalence of the first. In the
early Lagers, which were almost coeval with Hitler's coming
to power, work was purely persecutory, practically useless for
productive ends: to send the undernourished to dig up turf or
cut stone served only a terroristic purpose. At any rate, for
Nazi and Fascist rhetoric, in this the heir of bourgeois rhetoric,
'work ennobles', and therefore the ignoble adversaries of the
regime are not worthy of working in the commonly accepted

meaning of the word. Their work must be afflictive, must leave no room for professionalism, must be the work of beasts of burden – pull, push, carry weights, bend the back over the soil. This too is useless violence: useful only to break down current resistance and punish past resistance. The women of Ravensbrück tell about interminable days during the quarantine period (and before their incorporation in the factory work squads) which they spent shovelling sand dunes. In a circle, under the July sun, each deportee had to move the sand of her pile on to that of her neighbour on the right in a pointless and endless merry-go-round, because the sand ended up back where it came from.

But it is doubtful that this torment of body and spirit, mythical and Dantesque, was excogitated to prevent the formation of self-defence and active resistance nuclei: the Lager SS were obtuse brutes, not subtle demons. They had been raised to violence: violence ran in their veins, it was normal, obvious. It could be seen in their faces, their gestures, their language. To humiliate, to make the 'enemy' suffer, was their everyday task; they did not reason about it, they had no ulterior ends: their end was simply that. I do not mean to say that they were made of a perverse human substance, different from ours (there were also sadists and psychopaths among them, but they were few): simply enough, for a few years they had been subjected to a school in which current morality was turned upside down. In a totalitarian regime, education, propaganda and information do not meet with obstacles: they have an unlimited power, about which anyone who was born and has lived in a pluralistic regime will find it difficult to form an idea.

Unlike the purely persecutory labour, which I have just described, work could instead at times become a defence. It was so for the few in the Lager who were made to exercise their own trade: tailors, cobblers, carpenters, blacksmiths, bricklayers; such people, resuming their customary activity, recovered at the same time, to some extent, their human dignity. But it was also a defence for many others, an exercise of the mind, an escape from the thought of death, a way of living

day by day; in any case it is common experience that daily
cares, even though painful or irksome, help take one's mind
off more serious but more distant threats.

I frequently noticed in some of my companions (sometimes
even in myself) a curious phenomenon: the ambition of a 'job
well done' is so deeply rooted as to compel one 'to do well'
even enemy jobs, harmful to your people and your side, so
that a conscious effort is necessary to do them 'badly'. The
sabotage of Nazi work, besides being dangerous, also meant
overcoming atavistic inner resistances. The Fossano bricklayer who saved my life, and whom I described in *If This Is A
Man* and *Moments of Reprieve*, detested Germany, the Germans, their food, their language, their war; but when they set
him to build protective walls against the aerial bombs he built
them straight, solid, with well-staggered bricks and as much
mortar as was required; not in deference to orders but out of
professional dignity. In *A Day in the Life of Ivan Denisovich*
Solzhenitsyn describes an almost identical situation: Ivan,
the protagonist, sentenced, though guiltless, to ten years of
forced labour, finds satisfaction in building a wall according
to the highest standards of his trade, and then in realising
that it has turned out perfectly straight: Ivan '. . . was made
in that cretinous manner, nor had the eight years spent in
prison camps caused him to lose that habit: he valued everything and every job of work and would not let them be
spoiled unnecessarily.'

Those who saw the famous film, *The Bridge on the River
Kwai*, will remember the absurd zeal with which the English
officer, prisoner of the Japanese, strives to build an audacious
wooden bridge for them, and is shocked when he realises that
the English sappers have mined it. As one sees, love for a job
well done is a deeply ambiguous virtue. It animated Michel-
angelo through his last days, but also Stangl, that most
diligent Treblinka henchman, who answered an interviewer
with irritation: 'Everything I did of my own free will I had to
do as best I could. That's how I am.' Rudolph Höss, the
Auschwitz commander, boasts of the same virtue, when he

describes the creative travail that led to his invention of the gas chambers.

Finally I would like to mention, as an extreme example of at once stupid and symbolic violence, the iniquitous use that was made (not sporadically but with method) of the human body as an object, an anonymous thing belonging to no one, which one could dispose of in an arbitrary manner. About the medical experiments performed in Dachau, Auschwitz, Ravensbrück and elsewhere, much has already been written, and some of those responsible, who were not all physicians but often improvised as such, were even punished (not Josef Mengele, the most important and worst of all). The gamut of these experiments ranged from tests of new medications on unaware prisoners all the way to senseless and scientifically useless tortures, like those performed in Dachau, on Himmler's orders and on behalf of the Luftwaffe. Here, the chosen individuals, sometimes specially fed to be restored to their physiological normality, were subjected to long immersions in freezing water or introduced into decompression chambers in which air rarefaction at twenty thousand metres (an altitude that aircraft of the period were far from reaching!) was simulated in order to establish at what altitude human blood begins to boil: a datum that can be obtained in any laboratory at minimum expense and without victims, or can even be deduced from common tables.

It seems significant to me to recall these abominations at a time when, for good reason, there are discussions as to within what limits it is permissible to perform painful scientific experiments on laboratory animals. This cruelty, typical and devoid of apparent purposes but highly symbolic, was extended precisely because symbolic to the human remains after death: those remains which every civilisation, beginning with remotest prehistory, has respected, honoured and sometimes feared. The treatment to which they were subjected in the Lagers was intended to declare that these were not human remains but indifferent brute matter, in the best of cases good for some industrial use. After decades, horror and revulsion are still aroused by the display case in the Auschwitz Museum where the hair cut from the women sent to the gas chambers or the Lagers is exhibited pell-mell and by the ton: time has dis-coloured and macerated it, but it continues to whisper its mute accusation to the visitor. The Germans did not have the time to send it on to its destination: this unusual merchandise was purchased by a number of German textile industries which used it for the manufacture of mattress ticking and other indus-trial textiles. It is unlikely that those who utilised it did not know what sort of material this was. It is just as unlikely that the sellers, that is, the SS authorities of the Lager, actually made a profit from it: the outrage motive prevailed over the profit motive.

The human ashes coming from the crematoria, tons daily, were easily recognised as such, because they often contained teeth or vertebrae. Nevertheless, they were employed for several purposes: as fill for swamp lands, as thermal insulation between the walls of wooden buildings, as phosphate fertiliser; and especially notable, they were used instead of gravel to cover the paths of the SS village located near the camp. I couldn't say whether out of pure callousness or because, due to its origins, it was regarded as material to be trampled on.

I am under no illusion of having gone to the bottom of this question or of having demonstrated that useless cruelty is the exclusive appurtenance of the Third Reich and the necessary consequence of its ideological premises; what we know, for example, about Pol Pot's Cambodia suggests other explana-tions, but Cambodia is far from Europe and we know little about it, so how could we discuss it? Certainly, this was one of the fundamental features of Hitlerism not only inside the Lagers; and it seems to me that the best comment on it is summed up in these two remarks taken from a long interview by Gitta Sereny with the already mentioned Stangl, ex-commandant of Treblinka (*In quelle-tenebre*, Adelphi, Milan, 1975, p. 135).

'Considering that you were going to kill them all . . . what was the point of the humiliations, the cruelties?' the writer asks Stangl, imprisoned for life in the Düsseldorf gaol, and he replies: 'To condition those who were to be the material executors of the operations. To make it possible for them to do what they were doing.' In other words: before dying the victim must be degraded, so that the murderer will be less burdened by guilt. This is an explanation not devoid of logic but which shouts to heaven: it is the sole usefulness of useless violence.

# CHAPTER SIX

# The Intellectual in Auschwitz

To argue with a dead man is embarrassing and not very loyal. It is all the more so when the absent one is a potential friend and a most valuable interlocutor: but it can be an obligatory step. I speak about Hans Mayer, alias Jean Améry, the philosopher who committed suicide and a theoretician of suicide whom I have already quoted. Between these two names extends his life without peace and without a search for peace.

He was born in Vienna in 1912, in a family which was mainly Jewish but assimilated and integrated into the Austro-Hungarian empire. Even though nobody had converted to Christianity with the due formalities, Christmas was celebrated in his house around a tree adorned with shiny ornaments; on the occasion of small domestic accidents, his mother invoked Jesus, Joseph and Mary, and the souvenir photograph of his father who died at the front in the First World War did not show a wise, bearded Jew, but an officer in the uniform of the Tyrolean Kaiserjäger. Until he was nineteen years old, Hans had never heard about the existence of a Yiddish language.

He obtained his degree in literature and philosophy in Vienna, not without some collisions with the nascent National Socialist party: to him being Jewish was not important, but for the Nazis his opinions and tendencies had no weight whatsoever; blood is the only thing that matters, and his was impure enough to make him an enemy of Germanism. A Nazi fist broke one of his teeth, and the young intellectual was proud of the gap in his mouth, as if it were a scar received in a student duel. With the Nuremberg laws of 1935, and then the annexation of Austria by Germany in 1938, his fate was at a crossroads and the young Hans, a sceptic and pessimist by nature, did not delude himself. He was sufficiently lucid (*Luzidität* would always be one of his favourite words) to understand early on that in German hands every Jew is 'a dead man on vacation, a man to be murdered'.

He did not consider himself Jewish: he did not know Hebrew or Hebrew culture, did not heed the Zionist doctrine, religiously he was an agnostic. Neither did he feel able to construct for himself an identity he did not have: that would have been a falsification, a masquerade. Whoever is not born within the Jewish tradition is not a Jew, and cannot easily become one: by definition, a tradition is inherited; it is the product of centuries, it cannot be fabricated *a posteriori*. And yet, in order to live an identity – that is, dignity – is necessary. For him the two concepts coincided. Whoever loses one also loses the other, dies spiritually: without defences he is therefore exposed also to physical death. Now, to him, as to many other German Jews who like him believed in German culture, the German identity was denied by Nazi propaganda: on the obscene pages of Streicher's *Stürmer* the Jew is described as a hairy parasite, fat, with crooked legs, a beaked nose, flapping ears, good only at harming others. German he is not, by axiom; indeed, his presence is sufficient to contaminate public baths and even park benches.

From this degradation and this *Entwürdigung* it is impossible to protect oneself. The entire world watches it impassively. The German Jews themselves, almost all of them, succumbed to the state's abuses and felt objectively degraded. His way of escaping this was paradoxical and contradictory: to accept one's destiny, in this case Judaism, and at the same time rebel against the imposed choice. For the young Hans, a prodigal Jew, being Jewish was simultaneously impossible and obligatory; his ambivalence, which would follow him until death and indeed provoke it, begins here. He denied possessing physical courage, but he did not lack moral courage.

In 1938 he left his 'annexed' country and emigrated to Belgium. From now on he would be Jean Améry, almost an anagram of his original name. Out of dignity, and for no other reason, he accepted Judaism, but as a Jew '[he will not travel] through the world as a man afflicted by one of those diseases which do not cause great suffering but are certain to have a lethal end'. He, the cultivated German humanist and critic, tried to become a French writer (he would never succeed) and in Belgium joined a Resistance movement whose actual political hopes were negligible. His morality, for which he paid dearly in material and spiritual terms, by now has changed: symbolically at least it consists in 'returning the blow'.

In 1940, the Hitlerian tide submerged Belgium too and in 1943 Jean, who despite his choice remained a solitary and introverted intellectual, fell into the hands of the Gestapo. He was asked to reveal the names of his comrades and his superiors, otherwise he would be tortured. He is not a hero; in his pages he honestly admits that if he had known them he would have talked, but he did not know them. His hands were tied behind his back and he was hung by his wrists from a pulley. After a few seconds his arms came out of their sockets and remained twisted upwards, vertical behind his back. His torturers persevered. They savaged the hanging body which by now was unconscious, but Jean knew nothing, could not even take refuge in betrayal. He was healed, but identified as a Jew and sent to Monowitz-Auschwitz, the same Lager in which I too would be imprisoned a few months later.

Even though we never saw each other again, after liberation we exchanged several letters, having recognised, or, more accurately, come to know each other through our respective books. Our memories of down there coincide reasonably well on the plane of material details, but they diverge on one strange fact: I, who have always maintained that I preserve of Auschwitz a total, indelible memory, have forgotten his appearance; he declares that he remembers me, even though he confused me with Carlo Levi, who at that time was already well known in France as a political exile and painter. Indeed, he says that for a few weeks we lived in the same hut, and that he did not forget me because the Italians were so few as to constitute a rarity; furthermore, since in the Lager, during the last two months, I basically exercised my profession, that of chemist: and that this was an even greater rarity.

This essay of mine would like to be at once a summary, a paraphrase, a discussion and critique of *his* bitter and icy essay, which has two titles, *The Intellectual in Auschwitz* and *At the Limits of the Spirit*. It comes from a book that for many years I would have liked to translate. It too has two titles, *Beyond Guilt and Expiation* and *An Attempt to Overcome by One Overwhelmed*.

As one sees from the first title, the theme of Améry's essay is circumscribed with precision. Améry was in various Nazi prisons, and after Auschwitz he was briefly in Buchenwald and Bergen-Belsen, but his observations, for good reason, are confined to Auschwitz: the limits of the spirit, the non-imaginable, were there. Was being an intellectual in Auschwitz an advantage or a disadvantage? Of course it is necessary to define what is meant by intellectual. The definition proposed by Améry is typical and debatable:

I certainly do not mean to allude to all those who exercise one of the so-called intellectual professions: having received a good degree of education is perhaps a necessary condition but not sufficient. We all know lawyers, physicians, engineers, probably also philologists, who are certainly intelligent, perhaps even excellent in their field, but cannot be called intellectuals. An intellectual, as I would like it to be understood here, is a man who lives within a system of reference which is spiritual in the broadest sense. The sphere of his associations is essentially humanist and philosophical. His aesthetic consciousness is well developed. By inclination and aptitude he is attracted by abstract thought . . . If one talks to him about 'society', he understands the term in its sociological but not in its worldly sense. The physical phenomenon that produces a short-circuit does not interest him, but he

knows all about Neidhart von Reuenthal, that genteel
poet of the peasant world.

The definition seems to me pointlessly restrictive: more than
a definition it is a self-description, and from the context of
which it is a part I would not exclude a shade of irony:
in effect, to know von Reuenthal as Améry certainly knew
him was of little use in Auschwitz. I would say it is more
appropriate that in the term 'intellectual' be included, for
example, also the mathematician or the naturalist or the philosopher of science; what's more, it must be noted that in different countries the term takes on different colorations. But there
is no reason to split hairs; we do, after all, live in a Europe
which pretends to be united, and Améry's considerations
remain valid even though the concept under discussion is taken
in its larger sense; nor do I wish to follow in Améry's footsteps,
and pattern an alternative definition of my present condition.
(I may be an 'intellectual' today, even though the word fills me
with vague discomfort; I certainly was not one then, because
of moral immaturity, ignorance and alienation; and if I became
one later on, I paradoxically owe it precisely to the Lager
experience.) I would propose to extend the term to the person
educated beyond his daily trade; whose culture is alive inasmuch as it makes an effort to renew itself, increase itself and
keep up to date; and who does not react with indifference or
irritation when confronted by any branch of knowledge, even
though, obviously, he cannot cultivate all of them.

In any case, whichever definition one may choose, one can
only agree with Améry's conclusions. At work, which was
prevalently manual, the cultivated man was generally much
worse off than the uncultivated man. Aside from physical
strength, he lacked familiarity with the tools and the training
which his worker or peasant companion often had; in contrast,
he was tormented by an acute sense of humiliation and destitution – of *Entwürdigung*, that is, precisely, lost dignity.

I remember with precision my day of work in the Buna
plant. Even before adding our shipment of Italians (almost all

professional men or merchants) to the roster of the camp's population, they temporarily sent us to widen a large trench of clayey ground. They handed me a shovel and immediately it was a disaster: I was supposed to pick up the loose dirt at the bottom of the trench with the shovel and lift it over the edge which by now was more than two metres high. It seems easy and it is not: if one doesn't work with *élan*, and the correct *élan* at that, the loose dirt does not remain on the shovel but falls off, frequently on to the head of the inexperienced digger.

Also the 'civilian' foreman to whom we were assigned was temporary. He was a German past middle age who gave the impression of being a nice man and was sincerely shocked by our clumsiness. When we tried to explain to him that almost none of us had ever held a shovel, he shrugged his shoulders impatiently: what the hell, we were prisoners in zebra-striped clothes, and Jews besides. Everybody must work, because 'work makes free': isn't that what was written on the Lager's gate? This wasn't a joke; it was exactly so. Well, if we didn't know how to work, we only had to learn. Wasn't it true that we were capitalists? It served us right: today it's my turn, tomorrow yours. Some objected and received the first blows of their careers from the *Kapos* inspecting the area, others became despondent; others yet (I among them) confusedly perceived that there wasn't a way out, and that the best solution was to learn how to handle a pick and shovel.

Nevertheless, unlike Améry and others, my feeling of humiliation due to manual work was moderate: evidently I was still not 'intellectual' enough. And after all, why not? I had a degree, true enough, but mine was an undeserved piece of luck. My family had been rich enough to send me to school: many contemporaries of mine had shovelled dirt since adolescence. Did I not want equality? Well, then, I had got it. I was forced to change my opinion a few days later, when my hands and feet became covered with blisters and infections: no, you can't even improvise at being a digger. I had to learn a few fundamental things in a hurry, which the less fortunate (but in the Lager they were the most fortunate!) learn from childhood;

the correct way to grasp tools, the correct movements of arms and torso, how to handle fatigue and endure pain, knowing when to stop just before exhaustion, at the cost of being slapped and kicked by the *Kapos* and sometimes also by the German 'civilians' of the IG Farben works. Blows – I have said this elsewhere – are generally not lethal, but collapse is; a punch delivered skilfully contains its own anaesthesia, both corporal and spiritual.

Apart from work, barracks life was also more painful for the cultivated man. It was a Hobbesian life, a continuous war of everyone against everyone. (I repeat: this was Auschwitz, the concentrationary capital in 1944. Elsewhere, or at other periods, the situation may have been better, or perhaps even much worse.) The punch delivered by Authority could be accepted; it was, literally, a case of *force majeur*. Unacceptable on the other hand, because unexpected and irregular, were the blows received from fellow prisoners, which the civilised man rarely knew how to return. Furthermore, it was possible to find some dignity in manual labour, even in the most onerous, and it was possible to adjust to it, perhaps even by discerning in it a crude form of asceticism or, depending on temperament, a Conradian 'testing of oneself', a recognition of one's limits. Accepting barracks routine was much more difficult: making one's bed in the perfectionist and idiotic manner that I described as one of the useless violences, washing the wooden floor with filthy wet rags, dressing and undressing at a command, exhibiting oneself naked during the innumerable lice, scabies and personal cleanliness checks, making one's own the militaristic parody of 'close-order' drill, the 'eyes left' and 'caps off' briskly executed before the swinish belly of the SS NCO. This indeed was felt as a destitution, as a pernicious regression to a desolate state of infancy, bereft of teachers and love.

Améry-Mayer affirms also that he suffered from the mutilation of the language that I described in the fourth chapter: and yet his language was German. He suffered from it in a different way than we who, not knowing German, were reduced to the condition of deaf mutes: in a way, if I may put it like this, that was spiritual rather than material. He suffered from it *because* German was his language, because he was a philologist who loved his language: just as a sculptor would suffer at seeing one of his statues befouled or mutilated. Therefore the suffering of the intellectual was different in this case from that of the uncultivated foreigner. For the former, the German of the Lager was a language he did not understand and this endangered his life; for the latter, it was a barbaric jargon that he did understand but that scorched his mouth when he tried to speak it. One was a deportee, the other a stranger in his own country.

On the subject of blows among companions: in another of his essays Améry tells, not without amusement and retrospective pride, a key-episode that should be included in his *Zurückschlagen* or 'returning the blow' morality.

A gigantic Polish common criminal punched him in the face over some trifle; he, not because of an animal-like reaction but because of a reasoned revolt against the perverted world of the Lager, returned the blow as best he could. 'My dignity,' he says, 'was all in that punch aimed at his jaw; that in the end it was I who, physically much weaker, succumbed to a ruthless beating no longer had any importance whatsoever. Hurting all over from the blows, I was satisfied with myself.'

Here I must admit to my absolute inferiority: I have never known how to 'return the blow', not out of evangelic saintliness or intellectual aristocracy, but due to intrinsic incapacity – perhaps because of the lack of a serious political education. In fact, there does not exist a political programme, even the most moderate, even the least violent, that does not allow for some form of active defence. Perhaps because of a lack of physical courage: I possess a certain measure of it when confronted by natural dangers and disease, but I have always been bereft of it when confronted by a human being in the act of aggression. 'Trading punches' is an experience I do not have, as far back as I can go in memory; nor can I say I regret not having it. It is indeed because of this that my career as a Partisan was so brief, painful, stupid and tragic: I had taken on a role that was not mine. I admire Améry's change of heart, his courageous decision to leave the ivory tower and go down into the battlefield, but it was and still is, beyond my reach. I admire it: but I must point out that this choice, protracted throughout his post-Auschwitz existence, led him to positions of such severity and intransigence as to make him incapable of finding joy in life, indeed of living. Those who 'trade blows' with the entire world achieve dignity but pay a very high price for it, because they are sure to be defeated. Améry's suicide, which took place in Salzburg in 1978, like other suicides allows for a nebula of explanations, but, in hindsight, the episode of the defiance of the Pole offers one interpretation of it.

A few years ago I learned, in a letter to our common correspondent, Hety S., about whom I will speak later on, that Améry called me 'the forgiver'. I don't consider this either an insult or praise but an imprecision. I am not inclined to forgive, I never forgave our enemies of that time, nor do I feel I can forgive their imitators in Algeria, Vietnam, the Soviet Union, Chile, Argentina, Cambodia, and South Africa, because I know no human act that can erase a crime. I demand justice, but I am not able, personally, to trade punches or return the blows.

I tried to do so only once. Elias, the robust dwarf about whom I spoke in *If This Is A Man* and *Moments of Reprieve*, the man who to all appearances was 'happy in the Lager', had, I don't remember for what reason, seized me by the wrist and was insulting me and pushing me against a wall. Like Améry, I had a sudden upsurge of pride; conscious of betraying myself, and of transgressing a norm handed down to me by innumerable forebears alien to violence, I tried to defend myself and landed him a kick on the shin with my wooden clog. Elias roared, not from pain but from his wounded dignity. In a flash he crossed my arms over my chest and flung me to the ground, bringing all his weight to bear. Then he gripped my throat, attentively watching my face with eyes that I remember very well, at a hand's breadth from mine, fixed, a pale porcelain blue. He squeezed until he saw the signs of loss of consciousness begin; then, without a word, he let go and left.

Following this confirmation, whenever possible, I prefer to delegate punishments, revenges, and retaliations to the laws of my country. This is an obligatory choice: I know how badly these mechanisms function but I am the way I was made by my past and it is no longer possible for me to change. If I too had seen the world collapse upon me; if I had been sentenced to exile and the loss of national identity; if I too had been tortured until I fainted and lost consciousness and beyond, I would perhaps have learned to return the blow, and would harbour, like Améry, those 'resentments' to which he dedicated a long essay full of anguish.

These were culture's obvious disadvantages in Auschwitz. But weren't there really any advantages? I would be ungrateful for the modest (and 'dated') *liceo* and university education allotted to me by fate if I were to deny this; nor does Améry deny it. Culture could be useful: not often, not everywhere, not for everyone, but sometimes, on certain rare occasions, precious as a precious stone, it was actually useful, and one felt almost lifted up from the ground – with the danger of crashing back down again, the pain being all the greater the higher and longer the exaltation had lasted.

For example, Améry tells about a friend who in Dachau studied Maimonides. His friend was a male nurse in the ambulatory, and in Dachau, even though it was a very harsh Lager, there was a library, no less, while in Auschwitz even being able to glance at a newspaper was an unheard-of and dangerous event. He also tells that one evening, while marching back from work through the Polish mud, he tried to find again in certain verses by Hölderlin the poetic message which in other times had shaken him, but he didn't succeed: the verses were there, they sounded in his ear, but they no longer said anything to him; whereas at another moment (typically in the infirmary, having eaten an extra ration of soup during a respite from hunger) he had been filled with enthusiasm to the point of intoxication by evoking the figure of Joachim Ziemssen, the mortally ill but extremely dutiful officer in Thomas Mann's *Magic Mountain*.

Culture was useful to me; not always, at times perhaps by subterranean and unforeseen paths, but it served me well and perhaps it saved me. After forty years I am reading in *If This Is A Man* the chapter entitled 'The Canto of Ulysses'. It is one of the few episodes whose authenticity I have been able to verify (it is a reassuring operation: after a span of time, as I said in the first chapter, one can doubt one's memory) because my interlocutor of that time, Jean Samuel, is one of the book's few surviving characters. We remained friends, we met several times and his memories agree with mine: he remembers that conversation, but, so to speak, without accents or with shifted accents. At that time Dante did not interest him; I interested him by my naïve and presumptuous effort to transmit Dante, my language and my confused scholastic reminiscences to him in the space of half an hour and with the soup poles on our shoulders. Well, where I wrote 'I would give today's soup to know how to join, I had "none whatever" to the ending,' I had neither lied nor exaggerated. I really would have given bread and soup – that is, blood – to save from nothingness those memories which today with the sure support of printed paper I can refresh gratis whenever I wish, and which therefore seem of little value.

Then and there they had great value. They made it possible for me to re-establish a link with the past, saving it from oblivion and reinforcing my identity. They convinced me that my mind, though besieged by everyday necessities, had not ceased to function. They elevated me in my own eyes and those of my interlocutor. They granted me a respite ephemeral but not hebetudinous, in fact liberating and differentiating: in short, a way to find myself. Anyone who has read or seen *Fahrenheit 451* by Ray Bradbury can see what it would mean to be compelled to live in a world without books and what value the memory of books would assume in this world. For me, the Lager was this too. And before and after 'Ulysses' I remember having hounded my Italian companions so that they would help me retrieve this or that tatter of my past world, without getting much out of them, indeed reading irritation and suspicion in their eyes. What is this guy looking for with his Leopardi and the Avogadro's number?* Is hunger driving him crazy?

And I mustn't overlook the help I got from my trade as a chemist. On a practical plane, it probably saved me from at least several of the selections for the gas. From what I read afterwards on the subject (in particular in *The Crime and Punishment of IG-Farben* by J. Borkin), I learned that although it was under the jurisdiction of Auschwitz the Monowitz Lager was owned by the IG-Farben Industries, was in short a private Lager. The German industrialists, slightly less myopic than the Nazi commanders, realised that the specialists, to which category I belonged after passing the chemistry exam I was given, were not easily replaced. But I do not mean to refer here to this condition of privilege, nor to the obvious advantages of working under cover, without physical labour and without bullying *Kapos*: I refer here to a different advantage. I believe I can dispute, 'from personal experience', Améry's statement, which excludes scientists, and therefore with greater justification technicians, from the community of intellectuals: according to him these should be drawn exclusively from the fields of letters and philosophy. Was Leonardo da Vinci, who called himself 'a man without letters', not an intellectual?

Together with the baggage of practical notions I had got from my studies, I had brought along with me into the Lager an ill-defined patrimony of mental habits which derive from chemistry and its environs, but have broader applications. If I act in a certain way, how will the substance I hold in my hands react, or my human interlocutor? Why does it or he or she manifest or interrupt or change a specific behaviour? Can I anticipate what will happen around me in one minute or tomorrow or in a month? If so, which are the signs that matter,

* Number of molecules in a gram molecule.

which those to neglect? Can I foresee the blow, know from which side it will come, parry it, elude it?

But above all and more specifically: from my trade I contracted a habit that can be variously judged and defined at will as human or inhuman – the habit of never remaining indifferent to the individuals that chance brings before me. They are human beings, but also 'samples', specimens in a sealed envelope to be identified, analysed and weighed. Now, the sample book that Auschwitz had placed open before me was rich, varied and strange; made up of friends, neutrals and enemies, yet in any case food for my curiosity which some people, then and later, have judged to be detached. A food that certainly contributed to keeping a part of me alive and which subsequently supplied me with the material for thinking and making books. As I said, I don't know if down there I was an intellectual: perhaps I was so in flashes, when the pressure relented. If I became an intellectual afterwards, the experience I drew from it certainly helped. I know that this 'naturalistic' attitude does not derive only or even necessarily from chemistry, but in my case it did come from chemistry. On the other hand, and it should not seem cynical to say this for me, as for Lydia Rolfi and many other 'fortunate' survivors, the Lager was a university; it taught us to look around and to measure men.

From this aspect, my vision of the world was different from and complementary to that of my companion and antagonist Améry. A different interest transpires from his writings: that of the political combatant who enlisted because of the disease that plagued Europe and threatened (and still threatens) the world; that of the philosopher of the spirit, which in Auschwitz was absent; that of the diminished scholar from whom the forces of history have stripped away country and identity. Indeed, his gaze is directed on high and rarely lingers on the vulgar populace of the Lager, and on its typical character, the 'Muslim', the worn-out man, whose intellect is dying or dead.

So then, culture could be useful even if only in some marginal cases and for brief periods. It could enhance an hour, establish a fleeting bond with a companion, keep the mind alive and healthy; it definitely was not useful in orienting oneself and understanding. On this score my experience as a foreigner is identical to that of the German Améry. Reason, art, and poetry are no help in deciphering a place from which they are banned. In the daily life down there, made up of boredom and interwoven with horror, it was salutary to forget them, just as it was salutary to learn to forget home and family; I don't mean to speak of definitive oblivion of which, for all that, no one is capable, but of a relegation to that attic of memory where all the clutter of stuff that is no longer useful for everyday life is deposited.

A greater proclivity for this operation was shown by the uncultivated than by the cultivated. They adjusted sooner to that act of 'not trying to understand' which was the first wise dictum one had to learn in the Lager. To try and understand there, on the spot, was a futile effort, even for the many prisoners who came from other Lagers, or who, like Améry, knew history, logic, and morality, and what's more had experienced imprisonment and torture: a waste of energy that it would have been more useful to invest in the daily struggle against hunger and fatigue. Logic and morality made it impossible to accept an illogical and immoral reality: from this came a rejection of reality which as a rule rapidly led the cultivated man to despair. But the varieties of the man-animal are innumerable, and I saw and have described men of refined culture, especially if young, throw all this overboard, simplify and barbarise themselves and survive.

A simple man, accustomed not to ask questions of himself, was beyond the reach of the useless torment of asking himself why; besides, he often had a trade or a manual ability that facilitated his incorporation. It would be difficult to give a complete list because it varied from Lager to Lager and from moment to moment. As a matter of curiosity: in Auschwitz, in December 1944, with the Russians at the gates, the daily air raids and the ice that burst the pipes, a *Buchhalter-Kommando*, an accountants' squad, was instituted. The same Steinlauf, whom I described in the third chapter of *If This Is A Man*, was called to be part of it, but this was not enough to save him from death. Obviously this was an extreme case, to be placed within the general folly of the Third Reich's collapse yet it was normal and understandable that tailors, shoemakers, mechanics and bricklayers should find a good position; in fact they were too scarce. Indeed in Monowitz (certainly not for humanitarian reasons) a bricklayer's trade school was set up for prisoners below the age of eighteen.

The philosopher could also arrive at acceptance, says Améry, but by a longer route. He could perhaps break down the barrier of common sense that forbade him to accept a too ferocious reality as true; he could finally admit to living in a monstrous world, that monsters do exist, and that alongside Cartesian logic there existed the logic of the SS:

And what if those who proposed to annihilate him were right, on the basis of the undeniable fact that they were the stronger? Thus the fundamental spiritual tolerance and methodical doubt of the intellectual became factors of self-destruction. Yes, the SS were entitled to do what they did: natural right does not exist, and moral categories are born and die with fashions. There was a Germany that sent Jews and political adversaries to their death because it considered that only in this way could she realise herself. And so? Greek civilisation was also based on slavery, and an Athenian army set up its barracks in Melos just as the SS did in the Ukraine. Human victims were murdered in unheard-of numbers, so far as history's lights can illumine the past, and in any case the perennial quality of human progress was but a naïveté born in the nineteenth century. '*Links zwei drie drei vier*': the *Kapos*' command to mark step was a ritual like so many others. There is not much that one can oppose to horror: the Appian Way was bordered by two hedges of crucified slaves, and over Birkenau spread the fetid smell of burnt bodies. In the Lager the intellectual was no longer on the side of Crassus but on that of Spartacus: that's all there is to it.

\*

This surrender before the intrinsic horror of the past could lead the scholarly man to intellectual abdication, furnishing him at the same time with the defensive weapons of his un-cultivated companion: 'it always was like this, always will be like this.' Perhaps my ignorance of history protected me from this metamorphosis. Nor, on the other hand, to my good fortune, was I exposed to a further danger that Améry rightly mentions: by his very nature the intellectual (German, if I may be allowed to add this to his pronouncement) tends to become an accomplice of Power, and therefore approves of it. He tends to follow in Hegel's footsteps, and deify the State, any State; the sole fact of its existing justifies its existence. The chronicle of Hitlerian Germany teems with cases that confirm this tend-ency: to it have yielded, confirming it, the philosopher Hei-degger, Sartre's mentor; the physicist Stark, a Nobel Prize winner; Cardinal Faulhaber, the highest Catholic authority in Germany, and innumerable others.

Alongside this latent propensity of the agnostic intellectual, Améry observes what all of us ex-prisoners observed: the non-agnostic, the believers in any belief whatsoever, better resisted the seduction of power, provided, of course, they were not believers in the National Socialist doctrine. (This qualification is not superfluous: in the Lagers, and among those marked with the Red triangle of the political prisoner, there were also several convinced Nazis who had fallen from grace because of ideological dissidence or personal reasons. They were disliked by everyone.) When all is said and done, they also endured the trials of the Lager and survived in a proportionately higher number.

Like Améry, I too entered the Lager as a non-believer, and as a non-believer I was liberated and have lived to this day; actually, the experience of the Lager with its frightful iniquity has confirmed me in my laity. It has prevented me, and still prevents me, from conceiving of any form of providence or transcendent justice. Why were the moribund packed in cattle cars? Why were the children sent to the gas? I must nevertheless admit that I experienced (and again only once) the temptation to yield, to seek refuge in prayer. This happened in the October of 1944, in the one moment in which I lucidly perceived the imminence of death. Naked and compressed among my naked companions with my personal index card in hand, I was waiting to file past the 'commission' that with one glance would decide whether I should immediately go into the gas chamber or was instead strong enough to go on working. For one instant I felt the need to ask for help and asylum; then, despite my anguish, equanimity prevailed: you do not change the rules of the game at the end of the match, nor when you are losing. A prayer under these conditions would have been not only absurd (what rights could I claim? and from whom?) but blasphemous, obscene, laden with the greatest impiety of which a non-believer is capable. I rejected that temptation: I knew that otherwise were I to survive, I would have to be ashamed of it.

Not only during the crucial moments of the selection or the aerial bombings, but also in the grind of everyday life, the believers lived better: both Améry and I observed this. It was completely unimportant what their religious or political faith might be. Catholic or Reformed priests, rabbis of the various orthodoxies, militant Zionists, naïve or sophisticated Marxists and Jehovah's Witnesses – all held in common the saving force of their faith. Their universe was vaster than ours, more extended in space and time, above all more comprehensible. They had a key and a point of leverage, a millennial tomorrow so that there might be a sense to sacrificing themselves, a place in heaven or on earth where justice and compassion had won, or would win in a perhaps remote but certain future: Moscow, or the celestial or terrestrial Jerusalem. Their hunger was different from ours; it was a divine punishment or expiation, or votive offering, or the fruit of capitalist putrefaction. Sorrow, in them or around them, was decipherable, and therefore did not overflow into despair. They looked at us with commiseration, at times with contempt; some of them, in intervals of our labour, tried to evangelise us. But how can you, a layman, fabricate for yourself or accept on the spot an 'opportune' faith only because it is opportune?

In the fulgurating and very dense days that followed immediately after the Liberation, enacted against a pitiful scene of dying men, dead men, contaminated wind and polluted snow, the Russians sent me to the barber to be shaved for the first time in my new life as a free man. The barber was an ex-politico, a French worker of the *ceinture*. We immediately felt like brothers, and I made a few banal comments on our so improbable salvation: we were men sentenced to death and freed on the guillotine's platform, wasn't that true? He looked at me open-mouthed, and then exclaimed with deep disapproval: '*Mais Joseph était là!*' Joseph? It took me a few moments to realise that he referred to Stalin. He had not, he had never, despaired; Stalin was his fortress, the Rock sung in the psalms.

The demarcation between cultivated and uncultivated, of course, did not at all coincide with that between believers and non-believers: indeed, it cut across it at right-angles, forming four rather well-defined quadrants: the believing cultivated, the lay cultivated, the believing uncultivated, the lay uncultivated; four small jagged and coloured islands that stood out against the grey illimitable sea of the semi-alive who perhaps had been cultivated or believing, but by now no longer asked themselves any questions, and of whom it would have been useless and cruel to ask any questions.

The intellectual, Améry notes (and I would specify the young intellectual, which he and I were at the time of our capture and imprisonment), has drawn from his reading an odourless, ornate and literary image of death. I translate here 'into Italian' his observations as a German philologist, who must cite Goethe's 'More Light!', *Death in Venice*, and Tristan. For us in Italy, death is the second term of the binomial 'love and death'; it is Laura's, Ermengarda's and Clorinda's tender transfiguration; it is the sacrifice of the soldier in battle ('who for his country dies has lived greatly'); it is a 'beautiful death honours all of life'. This boundless archive of defensive and thaumaturgic formulations in Auschwitz (and also for that matter today in any hospital) was shortlived: *Death in Auschwitz* was trivial, bureaucratic, and an everyday affair. It was not commented on, it was not 'comforted by tears'. In the face of death, in the habit of death, the frontier between culture and lack of culture disappeared. Améry states that one no longer thought about *whether* one would die, an accepted fact, but rather about *how*:

> There were discussions about the time necessary for the poison in the gas chambers to take effect. There were speculations about the painfulness of death by phenol injection. Should one hope for a blow on the skull or death by exhaustion in the infirmary?

On this point, my experience and my recollections diverge from Améry's. Perhaps because I was younger, perhaps because I was more ignorant than he, or less marked, or less conscious, I almost never had the time to devote to death; I had many other things to keep me busy – find a bit of bread, avoid exhausting work, patch my shoes, steal a broom, or interpret the signs and faces around me. The aims of life are the best defence against death: and not only in the Lager.

# CHAPTER SEVEN

# Stereotypes

*I know, I know*

Those who experienced imprisonment (and, more generally, all persons who have gone through harsh experiences) are divided into two distinct categories, with rare intermediate shadings: those who remain silent and those who speak. Both obey valid reasons: those remain silent who feel more deeply that sense of malaise which I for simplicity's sake call 'shame', those who do not feel at peace with themselves, or whose wounds still burn. The others speak, and often speak a lot, obeying different impulses. They speak because, at varied levels of consciousness, they perceive in their (even though by now distant) imprisonment the centre of their life, the event that for good or evil has marked their entire existence. They speak because they know they are witnesses in a trial of planetary and epochal dimensions. They speak because (as a Yiddish saying goes) 'troubles overcome are good to tell'. Francesca tells Dante that there is 'no greater sorrow / than to recall happy times / in misery', but the contrary is also true, as all those who have returned know: it is good to sit surrounded by warmth, before food and wine, and remind oneself and others of the fatigue, the cold and hunger. In this manner, Ulysses immediately yields to the urgent need to tell his story before the table laden with food, at the court of the king of the Phaeacians. They speak, perhaps even exaggerating, as 'bragging soldiers', describing fear and courage, ruses, injuries, defeats, and some victories: by thus doing, they differentiate themselves from the 'others', consolidate their identity by belonging to a corporation and feel their prestige increased.

But they speak (in fact I can use the first person plural: I am not one of the taciturn), *we* speak also because we are invited to do so. Years ago, Norberto Bobbio wrote that the Nazi extermination camps were 'not *one of the* events, but *the* monstrous, perhaps unrepeatable event of human history'. The others, the listeners, friends, children, readers, or even strangers sense this, beyond their indignation and commiseration; they understand the uniqueness of our experience, or at least make an effort to understand it. So they urge us to speak and ask us questions, at times embarrassing us. It is not always easy to answer certain whys: we are neither historians nor philosophers but witnesses, and anyway who can say that the history of human events obeys rigorous logic, patterns. It is not said that each turn follows from a single why: simplifications are proper only for textbooks, the whys can be many, entangled with one another or unknowable, if not actually non-existent. No historian or epistemologist has yet proved that human history is a deterministic process.

Among the questions that are put to us there is one that is never absent; indeed, as the years go by, it is formulated with ever increasing persistence, and with an ever less hidden accent of accusation. More than a single question, it is a family of questions. Why did you not escape? Why did you not rebel? Why did you not avoid capture 'beforehand'? Precisely because of their inevitability, and their increase in time, these questions deserve attention.

The first comments on these questions, and their first interpretation, are optimistic. There exist countries in which freedom was never known, because the need man naturally feels for it comes after other much more pressing needs to resist cold, hunger, illnesses, parasites, animal and human aggressions. But in countries in which the elementary needs are satisfied, today's young people experience freedom as a good that one must in no case renounce: one cannot do without it, it is a natural and obvious right, and furthermore, it is gratuitous, like health and the air one breathes. The times and places where this congenital right is denied are perceived as distant, foreign and strange. Therefore, for them, the idea of imprisonment is firmly attached to the idea of flight or revolt. The prisoner's condition is perceived as illegitimate, abnormal: in short, as a disease which must be healed by escape or rebellion. In any case, the concept of escape as a moral obligation has strong roots. According to the military code of many countries, the prisoner-of-war is under the obligation to free himself at all costs, to resume his place as a combatant, and according to the Hague convention, the attempt to escape must not be punished. In the common consciousness, escape cleanses and wipes out the shame of imprisonment.

Let it be said in passing: in Stalin's Soviet Union the practice, if not the law, was different and much more dramatic. For the repatriated Soviet prisoner-of-war there was neither healing nor redemption; he was considered irremediably guilty even if he had managed to escape and rejoin the fighting army; he should have died instead of surrendering, and besides, having been (perhaps only for a few hours) in the hands of the enemy, he was automatically suspected of collusion with him. On their incautious return home, many military personnel who were captured by the Germans, dragged into occupied territory, and managed to escape and join the Partisan bands active against the Germans in Italy, France, or even behind the Russian lines, were deported to Siberia or even killed. In wartime Japan, the soldier who surrendered was regarded with great contempt; hence the extremely harsh treatment inflicted upon Allied military personnel who were taken prisoner by the Japanese. They were not only enemies, they were also cowardly enemies, degraded by their having surrendered.

More: the concept of escape as a moral duty and the obligatory consequence of captivity is constantly reinforced by romantic (*The Count of Monte Cristo!*) and popular literature (remember the extraordinary success of the memoirs of Papillon). In the universe of the cinema, the unjustly (or even justly) incarcerated hero is always a positive character, always trying to escape, even under the least credible circumstances, and the attempt is invariably crowned by success. Among the thousand films buried in oblivion, *I Am An Escaped Convict* and *Hurricane* remain in our memory. The typical prisoner is seen as a man of integrity, in full possession of his physical and moral vigour who, with the strength that is born of despair and ingenuity sharpened by necessity, flings himself against all barriers and overcomes or shatters them.

Now, this schematic image of prison and escape has little resemblance to the situation in the concentration camps. Using this term in its broadest sense (that is, in addition to the extermination camps, whose names are universally known, the many camps of military prisoners and internees also), there existed in Germany several million foreigners in a condition of slavery, overworked, despised, undernourished, badly clothed and badly cared for, cut off from all contact with their native land. They were not 'typical prisoners', they did not have integrity; on the contrary, they were demoralised and depleted. An exception should be made for the Allied prisoners-of-war (American and those belonging to the British Commonwealth) who received foodstuffs and clothing through the international Red Cross, had good military training, strong motivation and a firm *ésprit de corps* and had preserved a solid enough internal hierarchy exempt from the 'grey zone' which I mentioned before; but for a few exceptions, they could trust each other. They also knew that, should they be recaptured, they would be treated in accordance with international conventions. In fact, they attempted many escapes and some were carried through successfully.

For everyone else, the pariahs of the Nazi universe (among whom must be included gypsies and Soviet prisoners, both military and civilian, who racially were considered not much superior to the Jews), the situation was quite different. For them escape was both difficult and extremely dangerous. Besides being demoralised, they were weakened by hunger and maltreatment; they were, and knew they were, considered worth less than beasts of burden. Their heads were shaved, their filthy clothes were immediately recognisable, their wooden clogs made a swift and silent step impossible. If they were foreigners, they had neither acquaintances nor viable places of refuge in the surroundings; if they were German, they knew they were under careful surveillance and included in its files by the sharp-eyed secret police, and that very few among their countrymen would risk freedom or life to shelter them.

The particular (but numerically imposing) case of the Jews was the most tragic. Even admitting that they managed to get across the barbed wire barrier and the electrified grille, elude the patrols, the surveillance of the sentinels armed with machine-guns in the guard towers, the dogs trained for manhunts: in what direction could they flee? to whom could they turn for shelter? They were outside the world, men and women made of air. They no longer had a country (they had been deprived of their original citizenship) nor a home, confiscated for the benefit of the citizens in good standing. But for a few exceptions, they no longer had a family, or if some relative of theirs was still alive they did not know where to find him or where to write to him without putting the police on his tracks. Goebbels and Streicher's anti-Semitic propaganda had borne fruit: the great majority of Germans, and young people in particular, hated Jews, despised them, and considered them the enemies of the people; the rest, with very few heroic exceptions, abstained from any form of help because of fear of the Gestapo. Whoever sheltered or even simply assisted a Jew risked terrifying punishment. In this regard it is only right to remember that a few thousand Jews survived through the entire Hitlerian period, hidden in Germany and Poland in convents, cellars, and attics by citizens who were courageous, compassionate and above all sufficiently intelligent to observe for years the strictest discretion.

What's more, in all the Lagers the flight of even a single prisoner was considered the most grievous fault on the part of all the surveillance personnel, beginning with the functionary-prisoners and ending with the camp commander, who risked being discharged. In Nazi logic, this was an intolerable event: the escape of a slave, especially a slave belonging to races 'of inferior biological value', seemed to be charged with symbolic value, would represent a victory by one who by definition is defeated, a shattering of the myth; more realistically, it was also an objective damage since every prisoner had seen things that the world must not know. Consequently, when a prisoner was absent or did not respond at roll-call (a not very rare event: often it was simply a matter of a mistake in counting, or a prisoner who had fainted from exhaustion) apocalypse was unleashed. The entire camp was put in a state of alarm. Besides the SS in charge of surveillance, Gestapo patrols intervened; the Lager and its work sites, farm houses, and houses in the camp's environs were searched. The camp commander arbitrarily ordered emergency measures. The co-nationals or known friends or pallet neighbours of the fugitive were interrogated under torture and then killed; in fact, an escape was a difficult undertaking and it was unlikely that the fugitive had no accomplices or that his preparations had not been noticed. His hut companions, or at times all the prisoners in the camp, were made to stand in the roll-call clearing without any time limit, even for days, under snow, rain, or the hot sun until the fugitive was found, dead or alive. If he was tracked down and captured alive, he was invariably punished with death by public hanging. This hanging was preceded by a ceremony that varied from time to time, but was always of an unheard-of ferocity and in which the imaginative cruelty of the SS ran amok.

To illustrate how desperate an undertaking an escape was, but not only with this purpose in mind, I will here recall the exploit of Mala Zimetbaum; in fact I would like the memory of it to survive. Mala's escape from the women's Lager at Auschwitz-Birkenau has been told by several persons, but the details jibe. Mala was a young Polish Jewess who was captured in Belgium and spoke many languages fluently, therefore in Birkenau she acted as an interpreter and messenger and as such enjoyed a certain freedom of movement. She was generous and courageous; she had helped many of her companions and was loved by all of them. In the summer of 1944 she decided to escape with Edek, a Polish political prisoner. They not only wanted to reconquer their own freedom, but were also planning to document the daily massacre at Birkenau. They were able to corrupt an SS and procure two uniforms. They left in disguise and got as far as the Slovak border; here they were stopped by the customs agents, who suspected they were dealing with two deserters and handed them over to the police. They were immediately recognised and taken back to Birkenau. Edek was hanged right away, but refused to wait for his sentence to be read in obedience to the strict local ritual: he slipped his head into the noose and let himself drop from the stool.

Mala had also resolved to die her own death. While she was waiting in a cell to be interrogated, a companion was able to approach her and asked, 'How are things, Mala?' She answered: 'Things are always fine with me.' She had managed to conceal a razor blade on her body. At the foot of the gallows, she cut the artery on one of her wrists. The SS who acted as executioner tried to snatch the blade from her and Mala, under the eyes of all the women in the camp, slapped his face with her bloodied hand. Enraged, other guards immediately came running: a prisoner, a Jewess, a woman, had dared defy them! They trampled her to death; she expired, fortunately for her, on the cart taking her to the crematorium.

This was not 'useless violence'. It was useful: it served very well to crush at its inception any idea of escaping. It was normal for the new prisoners to think of escaping, unaware of these refined and tested techniques; it was extremely rare for such a thought to occur to the older prisoners; in fact it was common for escape preparations to be denounced by the members of the 'grey zone' or by third parties, afraid of the reprisals I have described.

I remember with a smile the adventure I had several years ago in a fifth grade classroom, where I had been invited to comment on my book and to answer the pupils' questions. An alert-looking little boy, apparently at the head of the class, asked me the obligatory question: 'But how come you didn't escape?' I briefly explained to him what I have written here; not quite convinced, he asked me to draw a sketch of the camp on the blackboard indicating the location of the watch towers, the gates, the barbed wire and the power station. I did my best, watched by thirty pairs of intent eyes. My interlocutor studied the drawings for a few instants, asked me for a few further clarifications, then he presented to me the plan he had worked out: here, at night, cut the throat of the sentinel; then, put on his clothes; immediately after this, run over there to the power station and cut off the electricity, so the search lights would go out and the high tension fence would be deactivated; after that I could leave without any trouble. He added seriously: 'If it should happen to you again, do as I told you; you'll see that you'll be able to do it.'

Within its limits, it seems to me that this episode illustrates quite well the gap that exists and grows wider every year between things as they were down there and things as they are represented by the current imagination fed by approximate books, films and myths. It slides fatally towards simplification and stereotype; I would like here to erect a dike against this trend. At the same time, however, I would like to point out that this is not a phenomenon confined to the perception of the near past and historical tragedies; it is much more general; it is part of our difficulty or inability to perceive the experience of others, which is all the more pronounced the further these experiences are from ours in time, space, or quality. We are prone to assimilate them to those 'related' ones, as though the hunger in Auschwitz were the same as that of someone who has skipped a meal, or as though escape from Treblinka were similar to an escape from any ordinary gaol. It is the task of the historian to bridge this gap, which widens as we get further away from events under examination.

With equal frequency, and an even harsher accusatory tone, we are asked: 'Why didn't you rebel?' This question is quantitatively different from the preceding one but similar in nature, and it too is based on a stereotype. It is advisable to answer it in two parts.

In the first place: it is not true that no rebellion ever took place in a Lager. The rebellions of Treblinka, Sobibor and Birkenau have been described many times, with an abundance of details; others took place in minor camps. These were exploits of extreme audacity worthy of the deepest respect, but not one of them ended in victory, if by victory one means the liberation of the camp. It would have been senseless to aim at such a goal: the excessive power of the guarding troops was such as to cause its failure within minutes, since the insurgents were practically unarmed. Their actual aim was to damage or destroy the death installations and permit the escape of the small nucleus of insurgents, something which at times (for example, in Treblinka, even though only in part) succeeded. However, there was never the thought of a mass escape: that would have been an insane undertaking. What sense, what use would it have been to open the gates for thousands of individuals barely able to drag themselves around, and for others who would not have known where, in an enemy country, to look for refuge?

Nevertheless there were insurrections; they were prepared with intelligence and incredible courage by resolute, still physically able minorities. They cost a fearful price in terms of human lives and the collective sufferings inflicted in reprisal, but served and still serve to prove that it is false to say that the prisoners of the German Lagers never tried to rebel. In the intentions of the insurgents, they were supposed to achieve another, more concrete result: bring the terrifying secret of the massacre to the attention of the free world. And indeed those few whose enterprise was successful, and who after many more depleting vicissitudes had access to the organs of information, did speak: but, as I mentioned in my introduction, they were almost never listened to or believed. Uncomfortable truths travel with difficulty.

In the second place: like the nexus imprisonment-flight, the nexus oppression-rebellion is also a stereotype. I don't mean to say that it is never valid: I'm saying that it is not always valid. The history of rebellions, that is, of insurrections or revolts from below by the 'many oppressed' against the few powerful, is as old as the history of humanity and just as varied and tragic. There were a few victorious rebellions, many were defeated, innumerable others were stifled at the start, so early as not to have left any trace in the chronicles. The variables in play are many: the numerical, military and idealistic strength of the rebels and, respectively, those of the challenged authority; the respective internal cohesions or splits; the external assistance available to one or the other; the ability, charisma or demonic power of the leaders; and luck. Yet, in every case, one can see that it is never the most oppressed individuals who stand at the head of movements: usually, in fact, revolutions are led by bold, open-minded leaders who throw themselves into the fray out of generosity (or perhaps ambition), even though they personally could have a secure and tranquil, perhaps even privileged life. The image so often repeated in monuments of the slave who breaks his heavy chain is rhetorical; his chains are broken by comrades whose shackles are lighter and looser.

This fact is not surprising. A leader must be efficient: he must possess moral and physical strength, and oppression, if pushed beyond a certain very low level, deteriorates both. To arouse anger and indignation, which are the motor forces of all true rebellions (to be clear about it, those from below; certainly not the putsches or 'palace revolts'), oppression must certainly exist, but it must be of modest proportions, or enforced inefficiently.

In the Lagers, oppression was of extreme proportions and enforced with the renowned and, in other fields, praiseworthy German efficiency. The typical prisoner, the one who represented the camp's core, was at the limits of depletion: hungry, weakened, covered with sores (especially on the feet: he was an 'impeded' man in the original sense of the word. This is not an unimportant detail!) and therefore profoundly downcast. He was a rag of a man, and, as Marx already knew, revolutions are not made in the real world with rags but only in the world of literary and cinematic rhetoric. All revolutions, those which have changed the direction of world history and those minuscule ones which we are dealing with here, were led by persons who knew oppression well, but not on their own skin. The Birkenau revolt, which I have already mentioned, was unleashed by the special Kommando attached to the crematoria: these were desperate, exasperated men but well fed, clothed and shod. The revolt in the Warsaw ghetto was an enterprise worthy of the most reverent admiration, it was the first European 'resistance' and the only one conducted without the slightest hope of victory or salvation; but it was the work of a political élite which, rightly, had reserved for itself a number of basic privileges in order to preserve its strength.

I come now to the third variant of the question: why didn't you run away 'before'? Before the borders were closed? Before the trap snapped shut? Here too I must point out that many persons threatened by Nazism and Fascism did leave 'before'. These were specifically political exiles, or intellectuals disliked by the two regimes: thousands of names, many obscure, some illustrious, such as Togliatti, Nenni, Saragat, Salvemini, Fermi, Emilio Segré, Lise Meitner, Arnaldo Momigliano, Thomas and Heinrich Mann, Arnold and Stefan Zweig, Brecht, and many others; not all of them returned, and it was a haemorrhage that bled Europe irremediably. Their emigration (to England, the United States, South America, and the Soviet Union; but also Belgium, Holland, France, where the Nazi tide was to catch up with them a few years later: they were, and all of us are, blind to the future) was neither flight nor desertion, but a natural joining up with potential or real allies, in citadels from which they could resume their struggle and their creative activity.

Nevertheless, it is still true that for the greater part the threatened families (the Jews, first of all) remained in Italy and Germany. To ask oneself and us why is once again the sign of a stereotyped and anachronistic conception of history; more simply put, of a widespread ignorance and forgetfulness, which tends to increase as the events recede further into the past. The Europe of 1930–1940 was not today's Europe. To emigrate is always painful; at that time it was also more difficult and more costly than it is now. To emigrate one needed not only a lot of money, but also a 'bridgehead' in the country of destination: relatives or friends willing to offer sponsorship and/or hospitality. Many Italians, peasants above all, had emigrated during the previous decades, but they were driven by poverty and hunger and had a bridgehead, or thought they did; often they were invited and well received because locally there was a scant supply of manual labourers. Nevertheless, for them and their families leaving their 'fatherland' was a traumatic decision.

*Patria* (that is, 'fatherland') – we would do well to examine this term. It is situated quite evidently outside the spoken language: no Italian, except for a joke, will ever say, 'I'll take the train and return to the fatherland.' The term was coined recently and does not have a single meaning; it does not have an exact equivalent in any languages other than Italian, it does not appear, so far as I know, in any of our dialects (and this is a sign of its erudite origin and its intrinsic abstraction), nor did it always have the same meaning in Italy. In fact, depending on the period, it indicated geographic entities of varying extension, ranging from the village where one is born and (etymologically) where our *padri* (fathers) lived, to the entire nation after the *Risorgimento*. In other countries it is more or less the equivalent of the hearth or birthplace; in France (and sometimes also among us) the term has taken on a connotation at once dramatic, polemical and rhetorical: the *Patrie* becomes such when it is threatened or spurned. For the man who goes away, the concept of *patria* becomes painful and also tends to fade; Pascoli, the poet, having left his Romagna, his 'sweet country' (not really going very far), sighed, 'My *patria* now is where one lives.' For Lucia Mondela, the woman in *The Betrothed*, *patria* is visibly identified with the 'uneven peaks' of her mountains rising from the waters of Lake Como. By contrast, in countries and times of intense mobility, such as now in the United States and the Soviet Union, there is no talk of *patria*, except in political-bureaucratic terms: what is the hearth, what is 'the land of the fathers', of those citizens eternally on the move? Many of them don't know, nor are they concerned about it.

But the Europe of the 1930s was very different indeed. Although industrialised it was still profoundly agricultural, or permanently urbanised. 'Abroad' for the great majority of the population was a remote and vague landscape, mainly for the middle class, less pressed by necessity. Confronted by the Hitlerian menace, the majority of indigenous Jews in Italy, France, Poland and Germany itself chose to remain in what they felt was their *patria* for reasons that to a great extent were held in common, albeit with different nuances from place to place.

Common to all were the organisational difficulties of emigrating. Those were times of grave international tension: the frontiers of Europe, today almost non-existent, were practically closed; Britain and the Americas admitted extremely reduced immigration quotas. Yet greater than this difficulty was another of an inner, psychological nature. This village or town or region or nation is mine; I was born here, my ancestors are buried here. I speak its language, have adopted its customs and culture; and to this culture I may even have contributed. I paid its tributes, observed its laws. I fought its battles, without caring whether they were just or unjust: I risked my life for its borders, some of my friends or relations lie in the war cemeteries. I myself, in deference to the current rhetoric, have declared myself willing to die for the *patria*. I do not want to nor can I leave it: if I die I will die 'in *patria*', that will be my way of dying 'for the *patria*'.

It is obvious that this sedentary and domestic rather than actively patriotic morality would not have stood up if European Judaism could have foreseen the future. It isn't that the premonitory symptoms of the slaughter were lacking. From his very first books and speeches Hitler had spoken clearly: the Jews (not only the German Jews) were the parasites of humanity and must be eliminated as noxious insects are eliminated. But, precisely, disquieting deductions have a difficult life: until the incursion of the Nazi (and Fascist) dervishes from house to house, one found a way to deny the signals, ignore the danger, manufacture those convenient truths of which I spoke in the first pages of this book.

This happened to a greater extent in Germany than in Italy. The German Jews were almost all bourgeois and they were German: like their 'Aryan' quasi-compatriots they loved law and order, and not only did they not foresee but they were organically incapable of conceiving of a terrorism directed by the state, even when it was already all around them. There is a famous, extremely dense verse by Christian Morgenstern, a bizarre Bavarian poet (not Jewish, despite his surname) which is quite apposite here, even though it was written in 1910, in the clean, upright and law-abiding Germany described by J. K. Jerome in *Three Men on the Bummel*. A verse so German and so pregnant that it has become a proverb and cannot be translated into Italian except by a clumsy paraphrase:

*Nicht sein kann, was nicht sein darf.*
(What may not be cannot be.)

This is the seal of a small emblematic poem: Palmström, an extremely law-abiding German citizen, is hit by a car in a street where traffic is forbidden. He gets up bruised and battered and thinks about it: if traffic is forbidden, vehicles may not circulate, *that is* they do not circulate. *Ergo* he cannot have been hit: it is 'an impossible reality', an *Unmögliche Tatsache* (this is the title of the poem). He must have only dreamed about it because, indeed, 'things whose existence is not morally permissible cannot exist'.

One must beware of hindsight and stereotypes. More generally one must beware of the error that consists in judging distant epochs and places with the yardstick that prevails in the here and now: an error all the more difficult to avoid as the distance in space and time increases. This is the reason why, for us who are not specialists, the comprehension of Biblical and Homeric texts or even the Greek and Latin classics is so arduous an undertaking. Many Europeans of that time, and not only Europeans and not only of that time, behaved and still behave like Palmström, denying the existence of things that ought not to exist. According to common sense, which Manzoni shrewdly distinguished from 'good sense', man when threatened provides, resists, or flees; but the threats of those days which today seem evident at that time were obfuscated by willed incredulity, mental blockages, generously exchanged and self-catalysing consolatory truths.

And here rises the obligatory question: a counter-question. How securely do we live, we men of the century's and millennium's end and, more specifically, we Europeans? We have been told, and there's no reason to doubt it, that for every human being on the planet an amount of nuclear explosive is stored equal to three or four tons of TNT; if even only one per cent of it were used there would immediately be tens of millions of dead, and frightening genetic damage to the entire human species, indeed to all life on earth, with the exception perhaps of the insects. Besides, it is to say the least probable that a third, generalised war, even conventional, even partial, would be fought on our territory between the Atlantic and the Urals, between the Mediterranean and the Arctic. The threat is different from that of the 1930s: less close but vaster; linked, in the opinion of some, to a demonism of History, new, still indecipherable, but not linked (until now) to human demonism. It is aimed at everyone, and therefore especially 'useless'.

So then? Are today's fears less or more founded than the fears of that time? When it comes to the future, we are just as blind as our fathers. Swiss and Swedes have their anti-nuclear shelters, but what will they find when they come out into the open? There are Polynesia, New Zealand, Terra del Fuego, the Antarctic: perhaps they will remain unharmed. Obtaining a passport and entry visa is much easier than it was then: so why aren't we gone, why aren't we leaving our country, why aren't we fleeing 'before'?

# CHAPTER EIGHT

# Letters from Germans

*If This Is A Man* is a book of modest dimensions, but, like a nomadic animal, for forty years now it has left behind it a long and intricate track. It was published for the first time in 1947, a run of 2,500 copies, and was well received by the critics but sold only in part: the six hundred unsold copies stored in Florence in a remainder warehouse were drowned in the autumn flood of 1969. After ten years of 'apparent death', it came back to life when the Einaudi publishing company accepted it in 1957. I have often asked myself a futile question: what would have happened if the book had immediately had a wide distribution? Perhaps nothing special: it is probable that I would have continued my hard-working life as a chemist who turned into a writer on Sunday (and not even every Sunday); or perhaps, on the other hand, I might have let myself be dazzled and, with who knows what luck, hoisted the banners of a life-sized writer. As I said, the question is futile: the business of reconstructing the hypothetical past, the what-would-have-happened-if is just as discredited as that of foreseeing the future.

Despite this false start, the book has made its way. It was translated into eight or nine languages, adapted for radio and theatre in Italy and abroad, discussed in innumerable schools. One stage of its itinerary was of fundamental importance for me: that of its translation into German and its publication in West Germany. When, around 1959, I heard that a German publisher (Fischer Bücherei) had acquired the translation rights I felt overwhelmed by the violent and new emotion of having won a battle. In fact I had written those pages without thinking of a specific recipient; for me, those were things I had inside, that occupied me and that I had to expel: tell them, indeed shout them from the rooftops. But the man who shouts from the rooftops addresses everyone and no one, he clamours in the desert. When I heard of that contract everything changed and became clear to me: yes, I had written the book in Italian, for Italians, for my children, for those who did not know, those who did not want to know, those who were not yet born, those who, willing or not, had assented to the offence; but its true recipients, those against whom the book was aimed like a gun were they, the Germans. Now the gun was loaded.

One must remember that only fifteen years had passed since Auschwitz: the Germans who would read me were 'those', not their heirs. Before they were oppressors or indifferent spectators, now they would be readers: I would corner them, tie them before a mirror. The hour had come to settle accounts, to put the cards on the table. Above all, the hour of conversation. I was not interested in revenge; I had been intimately satisfied by the symbolic, incomplete, tendentious, sacred representation in Nuremberg, but it was fine with me that the very just hangings should be taken care of by others, professionals. My task was to understand them. Not that handful of high-ranking culprits, but them, the people, those I had seen from close up, those from among whom the SS militia were recruited, and also those others, those who had believed, who not believing had kept silent, who did not have the frail courage to look into our eyes, throw us a piece of bread, whisper a human word. I remember very well that time and that climate, and I believe I can judge those Germans without prejudice or anger. Almost all, but not all, had been deaf, blind and dumb: a mass of 'invalids' surrounding a core of ferocious beasts. Almost all, though not all, had been cowardly. And right here, as a breath of fresh air and to prove how alien I am to global judgements, I would like to recount an episode: it was exceptional, and yet it happened.

In November 1944 we were at work in Auschwitz; together with two companions I was in the chemical laboratory I described elsewhere. The air raid alarm sounded and immediately the bombers were visible: there were hundreds, the raid promised to be monstrous. In the camp there were several large bunkers, but they were for the Germans and off limits to us. We had to make do with the fallow grounds by now already covered with snow, within the enclosure. All of us, prisoners and civilians, ran down the stairs headed for our respective destinations, but the head of the laboratory, a German technician, held us *Häftlinge* chemists back: 'You three come with me.' Astonished, we followed him at a run towards the bunker, but at the entrance stood a guard with a swastika on his armband. He said: 'You can go in; the others beat it.' The head of the laboratory answered: 'They are with me: it's either everyone or no one,' and tried to force his way inside. A boxing match ensued. The guard, who was a strong fellow, certainly would have won, but fortunately for everyone the all-clear sounded: the raid was not for us, the airplanes had continued north. If (another if! but how resist the fascination of bifurcated paths?), if anomalous Germans, capable of such modest courage, had been more numerous, that time's history and today's geography would be different.

I did not trust my German publisher. I wrote him an almost insolent letter: I warned him not to remove or change a single word in the text, and I insisted that he send me the manuscript of the translation in batches, chapter by chapter, as the work gradually proceeded. I wanted to check not merely on its lexical but also its inner faithfulness. Together with the first chapter, which I found very well translated, I received a letter in perfect Italian from the translator. The publisher had shown him my letter: I had nothing to fear, either from the publisher and even less from him. He introduced himself: he was exactly my age, had studied in Italy for several years, and besides being a translator he was an Italianist, a scholar who specialised in Goldoni. He too was an anomalous German. He had been called up for the army, but he found Nazism repugnant; in 1941 he had simulated an illness, had been sent to a hospital and had managed to spend his putative convalescence studying Italian literature at the University of Padua. He had then been given a deferral, remained in Padua and came into contact with the anti-Fascist groups led by Concetto Marchesi, Meneghetti and Pighin.

In September 1943, the Italian armistice had taken place, and in two days the Germans had militarily occupied Northern Italy. My translator had 'naturally' joined the Paduan partisans of the Justice and Liberty groups, who fought in the Colli Euganei against the Fascists of the Republic of Salò and against his compatriots. He had no doubts; he felt more Italian than German, a partisan and not a Nazi, and yet he knew what he was in for: hardships, dangers, suspicions and discomforts: if captured by the Germans (and he had in fact been informed that the SS was on his trail) an atrocious death; and moreover, in his own country he would be considered a deserter or even a traitor.

At the end of the war he settled in Berlin, which at that time was not split in two by the Wall, but governed by a very complicated condominium regime of the 'four big powers' of the time (the United States, the Soviet Union, Great Britain and France). After his Partisan adventure in Italy he was perfectly bi-lingual, spoke Italian without the trace of a foreign accent and began to do translations, first Goldoni because he loved him and because he knew the Venetian dialect well; and for the same reason Agnelo Beolco Il Ruzante, until then unknown in Germany; but also modern Italian authors, Collodi, Gadda, D'Arrigo and Pirandello. It was not well-paid work, or more accurately he was too scrupulous and therefore too slow for his working day to be justly recompensed; nevertheless, he could never make up his mind to take a steady job with a publisher. For two reasons: he loved his independence and besides, subtly, by indirect paths, his political past was held against him. Nobody ever told him in so many words, but a deserter, even in Bonn's super-democratic Germany, even in quadripartite Berlin was *persona non grata*.

He was enthusiastic about translating *If This Is A Man*:

he had an affinity with the book. By contrast, it substantiated his love for freedom and justice, translating it was a way to continue his daring and silent struggle against his misled country. At the time we were both too busy to travel, and a friendly exchange of letters sprang up between us. We were both perfectionists: he by profession; I because, although I had found an ally and a valuable ally, I was afraid that my text would lose colour, lose pregnancy. This was the first time that I was caught up in the always burning, never untaxing adventure of being translated, of seeing one's thoughts manhandled, refracted, one's painstakingly chosen word transformed or misunderstood, or even invigorated by some unhoped-for resource in the receiving language.

From the very first instalment I was able to see that in reality my 'political' suspicions were unfounded: my partner was as much an enemy of the Nazis as I, his indignation was as great as mine. There remained, however, the linguistic suspicions. As I mentioned in the chapter on communication, the German that my text needed, above all in dialogue and quotations, was much coarser than his. He, a man of letters and refined education, did in fact know the German of the barracks (after all he had had a few months of military service), but *per force* he did not know the degraded, often satanically ironic jargon of the concentration camps. Each of our letters contained a list of proposals and counter-proposals, and at times a vehement discussion was kindled over a single word. For example, the one I previously described. The pattern was general: I indicated a thesis to him, the one suggested to me by the acoustic memory to which I referred before; he presented me with an antithesis, 'this is not good German, today's readers would not understand it'; I retorted that 'down there we said exactly this'; finally we arrived at the synthesis, that is, a compromise. Experience then taught me that translation and compromise are synonymous, but at that time I was driven by a scruple of super-realism; I wanted that in that book, particularly in its German guise, nothing should be lost of its harshness and the violence inflicted on the language, which for that matter I had made an effort to reproduce as best I could in my Italian original. In a certain way, it was not a matter of a translation but rather of a restoration: his was, or wanted to be, a *restitutio in prisinum*, a retroversion to the language in which things had taken place and to which they belonged. More than a book, it should be a magnetic tape.

The translator understood quickly and well, and the result was an excellent translation from all points of view; of his fidelity I myself could be the judge, his stylistic flair was later praised by all reviewers. The question of a preface came up. Fischer, the publisher, asked me to write it myself. I hesitated, then I refused. I had a feeling of confused reluctance, repugnance, an emotional block that choked off the flow of ideas and words. In short, I was asked to append to the book – that is, to the testimony – a direct appeal to the German people, a peroration, a sermon. I was expected to raise my voice, climb on the podium, change from witness into judge, preacher; set forth theories and interpretations of history; divide or set apart the pious from the impious; pass from the third person to the second. All these were tasks that went beyond me, tasks I would gladly have delegated to others, perhaps the readers themselves, whether German or not.

I wrote to the publisher that I did not feel up to drafting a preface that would not denature the book, and I proposed an indirect solution to him: to place before the text, instead of an introduction, a passage from the letter which in May 1960, at the end of our laborious collaboration, I wrote to the translator to thank him for his work. I reproduce it here:

... And so we are finished: I am glad of it and satisfied with the result, grateful to you and also a little sad. You understand, it is the only book I have written, and now that we are finished transplanting it into German I feel like a father whose son has reached the age of consent and leaves and one can no longer look after him.

But it is not only this. Perhaps you have realised that for me the Lager, and having written about the Lager, was an important adventure that has profoundly modified me, given me maturity and a reason for life. Perhaps it is presumption: but there it is. Today I, prisoner No. 174517, by your help, can speak to the German people, remind them of what they have done, and say to them: 'I am alive, and I would like to understand you in order to judge you.'

I do not believe that man's life necessarily has a definite purpose; but if I think of my life and the aims I have until now set for myself, I recognise only one of them is well defined and conscious, and it is precisely this, to bear witness, to make my voice heard by the German people, to 'answer' the *Kapo* who cleaned his hand on my shoulder, Dr Pannwitz, and those who hanged Ultimo [these are people described in *If This Is A Man*], and by their heirs.

I am sure that you have not misunderstood me. I never harboured hatred for the German people. And if I had felt that way, I would be cured of it after having known you. I do not understand, I cannot tolerate the fact that a man should be judged not for what he is but because of the group to which he happens to belong ( . . . )

But I cannot say I understand the Germans: now, something one cannot understand constitutes a painful void, a puncture, a permanent stimulus that insists on being satisfied. I hope that this book will have some echo in Germany, not only out of ambition, but also because the nature of this echo will perhaps make it possible for me to better understand the Germans, placate this stimulus.

The publisher accepted my proposal, to which the translator had agreed with enthusiasm; so this page forms the introduction to all German editions of *If This Is A Man*: indeed, it is read as an integral part of the text. I became aware of this precisely because of the 'nature' of the echo to which I allude in the last lines.

\*

The echo takes material shape in about forty letters that were written to me by German readers during the years from 1961 to 1964: that is, during the crisis which led to the building of the Wall which to this day splits Berlin in two, and represents one of the most intense points of attrition in today's world: the only one, together with the Bering Strait, where Americans and Russians directly face each other. All these letters reflect an attentive reading of the book, but all of them answer, or attempt to answer, or deny there is an answer to, the question implicit in the last paragraph of my letter, that is, whether *it is possible to understand the Germans*. Other letters reached me piecemeal during the following years when the book was reprinted, but the more recent they are, the more pallid they become: the writers are by now the children and grandchildren, the trauma is no longer theirs, it is not being lived in the first person. They express vague solidarity, ignorance and detachment. For them, that past is truly the past, hearsay. They are not specifically German: with some exceptions, their letters could be confused with those I continue to receive from their Italian contemporaries, so I will not examine them in this review.

The first letters, those which count, are almost all from young people (who say they are or who appear to be young from the contents) with the exception of one which in 1962 was sent to me by Doctor T. H. of Hamburg and which I present here first because I am in a hurry to get rid of it. I translate its salient passages, respecting their clumsiness:

Dear Dr Levi,

Your book is the first among the stories by Auschwitz survivors that has come to our knowledge. It has deeply moved my wife and myself. Now, since you, after all the horrors you have lived, once again address the German people 'to understand', to 'awaken an echo', I will dare attempt an answer. But it will only be an echo; nobody can 'understand' such events!

... everything is to be feared from a man who is not with God: he has no brakes, no restraints! The word from *Genesis* 8.21 is then appropriate for him: 'Because the wisdom of the human heart is evil since youth', explained in modern times and proved by the dreadful discoveries of Freud's psychoanalysis in the field of the unconscious which certainly are known to you. In our times it has happened 'that the Devil was unleashed' without restraint, without meaning: persecutions of Jews and Christians, the extermination of entire populations in South America, of Indians in North America, of the Goths in Italy under Narses, horrendous persecutions and massacres during the French and Russian Revolutions. Who will be able to 'understand' all this?

But you certainly expect a specific answer to the question why Hitler came to power, and why afterwards we did not shake off the yoke. Now, in 1933 ... all moderate parties disappeared, and there remained only the choice between Hitler and Stalin, National Socialists and Communists, whose forces were approximately equal. We knew the Communists because of the large revolts that took place after the First World War. Hitler appeared suspect to us, it is true, but decisively as the lesser evil. That all his beautiful words were falsehood and betrayal we did not understand at the beginning. In foreign policy, he had one success after another; all states maintained diplomatic relations with him, the Pope was the first to make a concordat. Who could suspect that we were riding [sic] a criminal and a traitor? And, in any case, no guilt can certainly be attributed to the betrayed: the traitor alone is guilty.

And now the more difficult question, his insensate hatred for the Jews: well, this hatred was never popular. Germany deservedly counted as the country most friendly to the Jews in the entire world. Never, so far as I know and have read, during the Hitlerian period until its very end, did one ever hear of a single case of spontaneous outrage or aggression against a Jew. Always only (very dangerous) attempts of help.

Now I come to the second question. It is impossible to rebel against a totalitarian state. The entire world, when the time came, was unable to help the Hungarians. . . . Much less could we [resist] all by ourselves. It must not be forgotten that, aside from all the resistance struggles, on 20 July 1944, just on one day thousands and thousands of officers were executed. It certainly was not a matter of a 'small clique', as Hitler said afterwards.

Dear Dr Levi (I take the liberty to address you like this, because anyone who has read your book cannot but hold you dear), I have no excuses. I have no explanations. The guilt weighs heavily on my poor betrayed and misguided people. Rejoice for the life that has been given to you again, the peace of your beautiful country that I too know. Also Dante and Boccaccio have their place on my shelf. Your most devoted, T. H.

To this letter, probably without her husband's knowledge, Frau H. had added the following laconic lines which I also translate literally:

When a people realises too late that it has become a prisoner of the devil, from it follows certain psychic alterations.

1) All that is evil in men is stimulated. The results of this are the Pannwitzes and the *Kapos* who clean their hands on the shoulder of the defenceless.

2) From this results, in contrast, also the active resistance against injustice which sacrificed itself and its family [sic] to martyrdom but without visible success.

3) There remains the great mass of those who, to save their own lives, keep silent and abandon their brother in danger. This is what we recognise to be our guilt before God and mankind.

I often thought about this strange couple. He seems to me a

typical specimen of the large mass of the German upper middle class: a not fanatical but opportunistic Nazi who repented when it was opportune to repent, stupid enough to believe that he can make me believe his simplified version of recent history and dares to have recourse to Narses's and the Goths' retroactive reprisals. She seems to me a little less hypocritical than her husband but more bigoted.

I answered with a long letter, perhaps the only irate one I ever wrote. That no Church offers indulgences to those who follow the Devil or accepts as justification the attribution of one's sins to the Devil. That one must answer personally for sins and errors, otherwise all trace of civilisation would vanish from the face of the earth, as in fact it had vanished from the Third Reich. That his electoral data might be good for a child: in the elections of November 1932, the last to be freely held, the Nazis, true enough, obtained 196 seats in the Reichstag, but alongside the Communists with one hundred seats, the Social Democrats, who certainly were not extremists and indeed were detested by Stalin, had obtained 120. That, above all, on *my* shelf next to Dante and Boccaccio I keep my *Mein Kampf*, 'My Struggle', written by Adolf Hitler many years before coming to power. That dread man was not a traitor, he was a coherent fanatic whose ideas were extremely clear: he never changed them and never concealed them. Those who voted for him certainly voted for his ideas. Nothing is lacking in that book: the blood and the land, the living space, the Jew as the eternal enemy, the Germans who embody 'the highest form of humanity on earth', the other countries openly regarded as the instruments of German domination. These are not 'beautiful words'; perhaps Hitler also uttered other words, but he never retracted these.

As for the German resistors, all honour to them but to tell the truth the conspirators of 20 July 1944 bestirred themselves a bit too late. And, finally, I wrote:

Your most audacious statement is the one regarding the unpopularity of anti-Semitism in Germany. It was the foundation of Nazi doctrine from its beginnings: it was of a mystical nature, the Jews could not be 'the people elected by God' since that's what the Germans were. There's neither a page nor a speech of Hitler's in which hatred against the Jews is not reiterated to the point of obsession. It was not marginal to Nazism: it was its ideological centre. And so: how could the people 'most friendly toward the Jews' vote for the party and praise the man who called the Jews Germany's first enemy and claimed that the prime objective of their politics was 'strangling the Judaic hydra'?

As for outrages and spontaneous aggressions, your sentence is truly outrageous. In the face of millions of dead people, it seems idle and odious to discuss whether or not it was a matter of spontaneous persecution: and in any case, Germans are not much inclined to spontaneity. But I might remind you that nothing obliged German industrialists to hire famished slaves if not their profit; that no one forced the Topf Company (flourishing today in Wiesbaden) to build the enormous multiple crematoria in the Lagers; that perhaps the SS did receive orders to kill the Jews, but enrolment in the SS was voluntary; that I myself found in Katowitz, after the liberation, innumerable packages of forms by which the heads of German families were authorised to draw clothes and shoes for *adults and for children* from the Auschwitz warehouses; did no one ask himself where so many children's shoes were coming from? And did you never hear about a certain Crystal Night? Or do you think that each single crime committed that night was imposed by force of the law?

That there were attempts to help, I know, and I know that they were dangerous; and in the same way, having lived in Italy, I know 'that it is impossible to rebel in a totalitarian state'; but I know that there exist a thousand ways, much less dangerous, to manifest one's solidarity with the oppressed, that these were frequent in

Italy even after the German occupation, and that in Hitler's Germany they were carried out much too infrequently.

The remaining letters are very different: they delineate a better world. But I must point out that, even with the best will to absolve, they cannot be considered a 'representative sample' of the German people of that time. In the first place, that book of mine was published in some tens of thousands of copies and was therefore read by one out of every thousand citizens of the Federal Republic: a few must have bought it by chance, the rest because they were somehow predisposed for the collision with facts, sensitised, permeable. Among these readers only about forty, as I mentioned, decided to write to me.

In forty years of practice, I have by now become familiar with this singular personage, the reader who writes to the author. He can belong to one of two clearly distinct constellations, one pleasing, the other disagreeable; the intermediary instances are rare. The former give joy and teach. They have read the book attentively, often more than once; they have loved and understood it, at times better than the author himself; they declare themselves enriched by it; present their views with great clarity and occasionally their criticism; they thank the author for his work; often they explicitly exempt him from writing a reply. The latter are irksome and a waste of time. They exhibit themselves; parade their merits; often have manuscripts in their drawer, and let it become clear that their intention is to climb with the help of the book and the author, as ivy climbs up tree trunks; or they may also be children or adolescents who write out of bravado, on a bet, to obtain an autograph. My forty German correspondents, to whom I dedicate these pages with gratitude all belong (except for the Doctor T. H. mentioned earlier, who is a case apart) to the first constellation.

L. I. is a librarian in Westphalia; she confesses to having been violently tempted to close the book half-way through 'to escape the images evoked in it', but was immediately ashamed of this selfish and cowardly impulse. She writes:

> In your preface you express the desire to understand us Germans. You must believe us when we tell you that we ourselves are incapable of conceiving of ourselves or of what we have done. We are guilty. I was born in 1922, grew up in Upper Silesia, not far from Auschwitz, but at the time, in truth, I knew nothing (please do not consider this statement as a convenient excuse, but as a fact) of the atrocious things that were being committed, actually a few kilometres away from us. And yet, at least until the outbreak of the war, I happened to meet here and there people with the Jewish star and I did not welcome them into my home nor did I offer them hospitality as I would have done with others, did not intervene on their behalf. That is my crime. I can come to terms with this terrible levity of mine, cowardice and selfishness only by relying on Christian forgiveness.

Furthermore, she says she is a member of *Aktion Sühnezeichen* (Expiatory Action), an evangelical association of young people who spend their vacations abroad, rebuilding the cities most grievously damaged by the German war (she went to Coventry). She says nothing about her parents, and this is a symptom: either they knew and did not talk to her; or they did not know, and in that case they had not talked to those who down there must certainly have known – the railroad personnel of the convoys, the warehouse workers, the thousands of German workers in the factories and mines where the slave-workers were worked to death, in short, anyone who did not hold his hand over his eyes. I repeat: the true crime, the collective, general crime of almost all Germans of that time was that of lacking the courage to speak.

M. S. from Frankfurt says nothing about himself and cautiously searches for distinctions and justifications: this too is a symptom.

You write that you do not understand the Germans . . .
As a German, sensitive to the horror and shame and who
will continue to be aware until the end of his days that
the horror itself took place by the hand of men of his
country, I feel called upon directly by your words and
wish to reply.

I too do not understand men like that *Kapo* who wiped
his hand on your shoulder, men like Pannwitz, like
Eichmann, and all the others who executed inhuman
orders without realising that one cannot evade one's own
responsibility by hiding behind that of others. Or that in
Germany there were so many material executors of a
criminal system and that all this could take place precisely
thanks to the great number of people thus disposed and
willing, who would not, insofar as they were German, be
afflicted by all this.

But are they 'the Germans'? and is it permissible in any
case to speak of 'Germans' as a single entity, or 'English'
or 'Italians' or 'Jews'? You mentioned certain exceptions
to the Germans whom you do not understand . . .: I thank
you for these words of yours, but I beg you to remember
the innumerable Germans . . . who suffered and died in
their struggle against iniquity . . .

With all my heart I wish that many of my compatriots
will read your book, so that we Germans will not become
lazy and indifferent, but on the contrary that there will
remain vivid in us the awareness of how low man can fall
when he becomes a torturer of his fellow man. If this will
happen, your book will contribute to all this never
happening again.

I answered M. S. with perplexity: the same perplexity, for
that matter, which I experienced in answering all these polite
and civil interlocutors, members of a people who exterminated
mine (and many others). What is at stake, essentially, is
the same embarrassment experienced by dogs studied by
neurologists, conditioned to react in one way to the circle and

in another way to the square, so that when the square became
rounded and began to resemble a circle, the dogs were blocked
and presented the signs of neurosis. I wrote to him, among
other things:

> I agree with you: it is dangerous, wrong, to speak about
> the 'Germans', or any other people as of a single undif-
> ferentiated entity, and include all individuals in one judge-
> ment. And yet I don't think I would deny that there exists
> a spirit of each people (otherwise it would not be a people),
> a *Deutschtum*, an *Italianita*, an *Hispanidad*: they are the
> sums of traditions, customs, history, language and culture.
> Whoever does not feel within himself this spirit, which is
> national in the best sense of the word, not only does not
> entirely belong to his own people but he is not part of
> human civilisation. Therefore, while I consider insensate
> the syllogism: 'All Italians are passionate; you are Italian;
> therefore you are passionate'; I do, however, believe it
> legitimate, within certain limits, to expect from Italians
> taken as a whole, or from Germans, etc., one specific,
> collective behaviour rather than another. There will cer-
> tainly be individual exceptions, but a prudent, probab-
> ilistic forecast is in my opinion possible . . .
>   . . . I will be honest with you: in the generation that is
> over forty-five, how many are the Germans truly con-
> scious of what happened in Europe in the name of
> Germany? To judge from the disconcerting outcome of a
> number of trials, I feel they are few: along with heart-
> broken and compassionate voices, I hear others, dis-
> cordant, strident, too proud of the power and wealth of
> today's Germany.

I. J. from Stuttgart is a social worker. She says:

> That you were able to prevent an irremediable hatred
> against us Germans from seeping through your writings
> is truly a miracle and should induce us to shame. For

this I would like to thank you. Unfortunately there are still among us many who refuse to believe that we Germans really committed such inhuman horrors against the Jewish people. Naturally, this denial springs from many diverse motives, perhaps even only from the fact that the intellect of the average citizen refuses to consider the possibility of such profound evil among us 'Western Christians'.

It is good that your book was published here and can thus bring light to many young people. It will also be possible to put it in the hands of some older people, but to do this, in our 'sleeping' Germany, a certain amount of civil courage is necessary.

I answered her:

That I do not feel hatred against the German surprises many, and it should not. In reality, I do understand hatred, but only *ad personam*. If I were a judge, even though repressing what hatred I might feel, I would not hesitate to inflict the most severe punishment or even death on the many culprits who still today live undisturbed on German soil or in other countries of suspect hospitality; but I would experience horror if a single innocent were punished for a crime he did not commit.

W. A., a physician, writes from Würtemberg:

For us Germans, who carry the heavy burden of our past and (God knows!) of our future, your book is more than a moving tale: it is a help. It is an orientation for which I thank you. I can say nothing to exculpate us; nor do I believe that culpability (*this* culpability!) can easily be obliterated ... Much though I try to remove myself from the evil spirit of the past, I still remain a member of this people whom I love and who in the course of centuries has given birth in equal measure to works of noble peace and to others filled with demonic peril. In this converging of all the different times in our history, I am conscious of being implicated in the greatness and culpability of my people. I therefore stand before you as an accomplice of those who did violence to your destiny and the destiny of your people.

W. G. was born in 1935 in Bremen; he is a historian and sociologist, a militant member of the Social Democratic Party:

... At the end of the war I was still a child; I cannot take upon myself any share of guilt for the frightful crimes committed by Germans; and yet I am ashamed of them; I hate the criminals who made you and your companions suffer, and I hate their accomplices, many of whom are still alive. You write that you cannot understand the Germans. If it is your intention to allude to the executioners and their helpers, then I too cannot understand them; but I hope I will have the strength to fight them if they should appear again on the stage of history. I spoke of 'shame': I meant to express this feeling – that what was perpetrated by German hands at that time should never have happened, nor should it have been approved of by other Germans.

With H. L. from Bavaria, a student, matters became complicated. She wrote to me for the first time in 1962; her letter was singularly alive, free of the leaden gloom that characterises almost all the others, even the best intentioned. She assumed that I expected 'an echo' above all from important official persons, not from a young girl, but 'she feels called upon personally as heir and accomplice'. She is satisfied with the education she receives in school, and with what she has been taught about her country's recent history, but she is not sure 'that one day the lack of measure that is typical of Germans will not explode again, in a different guise, and directed at other goals'. She deplores the fact that her contemporaries reject politics as 'something dirty'. She reacted in a 'violent and rude manner' to a priest who maligned the Jews and to her Russian teacher, a Russian woman who claimed the Jews were responsible for the October Revolution and considered the Hitlerian slaughter a just punishment. At such moments, she experienced 'an indescribable shame at belonging to the most barbaric of peoples'. 'Even though outside all mysticism or superstition,' she is convinced 'that we Germans will not escape a just punishment for what we committed'. She feels somehow authorised, indeed duty-bound to declare that 'we, the children of a generation laden with guilt, are fully conscious of it, and will try to alleviate yesterday's horrors and sufferings so as to avoid their being repeated tomorrow'.

Since she seemed to me an intelligent, unprejudiced and 'new' interlocutor, I wrote and asked her for more precise information about the situation of the Germany of that time (this was the Adenauer period); as for her fear of a collective 'just punishment', I tried to convince her that a punishment, if it is collective, cannot be just, and vice versa. By return post she sent me a card on which she told me that my questions required a certain amount of research; I should be patient, she would answer me exhaustively as soon as possible. Twenty days later I received from her a twenty-three-page letter: in short, a thesis, compiled thanks to a frenzied work of interviews which she carried out by phone and letter. So this nice girl too, even though for a good end, had a propensity for *Masslosigkeit*, that lack of measure she herself had denounced, but with comical sincerity she apologised: 'I didn't have much time, so many things that I could have said more briefly remained as they were.' Since I am not *masslos* I confine myself to summing up and quoting the passages which to me seem most significant.

> ... I love the country where I've grown up, I adore my
> mother, but despite my efforts the German as a particular
> human type does not appeal to me: perhaps because he
> still seems to be too marked by those qualities which in

the recent past manifested themselves so rigorously, but perhaps also because in it I detest myself, recognising that in essence I am like him.

To a question of mine about the school, she answers (with documents) that the entire teaching body was at the proper time put through the sieve of 'de-Nazification' demanded by the Allies, but conducted in an amateurish, dilettantesque manner and widely sabotaged. Nor could it have been otherwise: an entire generation would have had to be banished. Recent history is being taught in the schools, but there is little talk about politics. The Nazi past surfaces here and there in varying tones: a few professors boast about it, a few hide it, very few declare themselves immune from it. A young teacher has declared to her as follows:

Pupils are not very interested in this period, but immediately pass to the opposition if one speaks to them about a collective German guilt. Many indeed state that they've had enough of the *mea culpa* of the press and their teachers.

H. L. comments:

. . . It is precisely in the resistance of the young people to the *mea culpa* that one can see how, for them, the problem of the Third Reich remains just as unresolved, irritating and typically German as for those who lived before them. Only when this emotionalism has ceased will it be possible to reason objectively.

Elsewhere, speaking of her own experience, H. L. writes (very plausibly):

The professors did not avoid the problems; on the contrary, documenting them with newspapers of the period, they demonstrated the propaganda methods of the Nazis.

They told how, when they were young, they had followed the new movement without criticisms and with enthusiasm: youth rallies, sports organisations, etc. We students attacked them strongly, wrongly as I think today: how can one accuse them of having understood the situation, and foreseen the future, behaving no better than the adults? And we, in their place, would we have unmasked better than they the satanic methods with which Hitler conquered the youth for his war?

It should be noted: the justification is the same as that put forward by Doctor T. H. of Hamburg, and at any rate no witness of the time ever denied Hitler a truly demonic talent for persuading, the same talent that favoured him in his political contacts. It can be accepted from young people who, understandably, try to exculpate their fathers' entire generation; not from the older people compromised and falsely penitent who try to limit the guilt to a single man.

H. L. sent me many more letters, arousing in me bifidous reactions. She described her father for me, a restless musician, shy and sensitive, who died when she was a little girl: was she searching for a father in me? She swayed between documentary seriousness and childish fantasy. She sent me a kaleidoscope and with it she wrote:

... About you too I have constructed for myself a well-defined image: it is you who, having escaped a terrifying destiny (forgive my presumption), wanders about our country, still estranged, as in a bad dream. I thought I ought to sew a suit for you like those donned by the heroes of legend, a suit that will protect you from all the world's dangers.

I could not recognise myself in this image but I did not tell her that. I answered that such suits cannot be given away as gifts: one must weave and sew them for oneself. H. L. sent me two novels of Heinrich Mann's *Henry IV* cycle, which unfortunately I never found the time to read; I arranged for her to receive the German translation of *The Truce*, which had appeared in the meantime. In December 1964, from Berlin where she had moved, she sent me a pair of gold cuff-links made by a girlfriend of hers who was a goldsmith. I did not have the heart to return them; I thanked her but asked her not to send me anything else. I sincerely hope I did not offend this intimately gentle person; I hope she understood the reason for my defensiveness. Since then I have received no further news from her.

I have left for last my exchange of letters with Mrs Hety S. of Wiesbaden, my contemporary, because it represents an episode apart both in quality and quantity. By itself, my H. S. dossier is more voluminous than that in which I keep all the other 'letters from Germans'. Our correspondence extends over sixteen years, from October 1966 to November 1982. It contains, besides about fifty of her letters (often four or more pages long) and my answers, also the onion skins of at least as many letters she wrote to her children, to friends, to other writers, publishers, local organisations, newspapers or magazines, copies of which she considered important enough to send me; and, finally, newspaper clippings and book reviews. Some of her letters are 'circulars': a half-page is a photocopy, the same for several correspondents, the rest is blank and filled in by hand with more personal information or questions. Mrs Hety S. wrote to me in German and did not know Italian; at first I answered her in French, then I realised that she understood it with difficulty and for a long time I wrote to her in English. Later, with her amused consent, I wrote to her in my uncertain German, in duplicate; she would return one copy to me with her corrections, carefully explained. We met only twice: at her house during a hurried business trip of mine to Germany, and in Turin during just as hurried a vacation of hers. These were not important encounters: the letters count for much more.

Her first letter took as its point of departure the question of 'understanding', but it had an energetic, resentful tone that distinguished it from all the others. My book had been given to her as a gift by a common friend, the historian Hermann Langbein, but very late, when the first edition was already exhausted. As cultural assessor of a regional government, she was trying to have it reprinted immediately and wrote to me:

> You will certainly never be able to understand 'the Germans': even we are unable to do so, because at that time there happened things that, under no circumstances, should have happened. As a result, for many among us words like 'Germany' and 'Fatherland' have forever lost the meaning they once had: the concept of the 'Fatherland' has been obliterated for us ... What absolutely is not permissible is to forget. Hence for the new generation books like yours that describe the inhuman in such a human manner are important ... Perhaps you do not fully realise how many things a writer can implicitly express about himself – and thus about Man in general. It is precisely this that confers weight and value to every chapter of your book. More than all the rest, I was dismayed by your pages on the Buna laboratory: this then was how you prisoners saw us free people!

A little further on, she tells about a Russian prisoner who during the winter delivered coal to her cellar. Speaking to him was forbidden: she slipped food and cigarettes into his pocket, and he to thank her shouted: 'Heil Hitler!' On the other hand, she was not forbidden (what a labyrinth of hierarchies and differentiating prohibitions the Germany of that time must have been! and the 'letters from Germans' and hers in particular say more than one might think) to speak with a young French 'volunteer' worker: she would pick her up at her camp, bring her home, even take her to a few concerts. In camp the girl was unable to wash herself properly and she had lice. Hety did not dare tell her. She felt embarrassed and was ashamed of her embarrassment.

To this first letter of hers I answered that my book had, it is true, awakened some resonance in Germany, but actually among the Germans who least needed to read it: I had received penitent letters from the innocent, not the guilty. These, understandably, were silent.

In her subsequent letters, little by little, in her indirect way, Hety (for the sake of simplicity I will refer to her like this even though we never reached a first name footing) gave me a portrait of herself. Her father, a pedagogue by profession, was a Social Democratic activist as early as 1919; in 1933, the year in which Hitler seized power, he immediately lost his job, perquisitions and financial difficulties followed. The family was forced to move to smaller lodgings. In 1935 Hety was expelled from her school because she had refused to become a member of the Hitler Youth Organisation. In 1938 she married an IG-Farben engineer (hence her interest in 'the Buna laboratory'!) by whom she immediately had two children. After the attempt on Hitler's life on 20 July 1944, her father was deported to Dachau, and her marriage underwent a crisis because her husband, even though he wasn't a Party member, would not tolerate Hety's endangering herself, him, and the children in order to 'do what must be done', that is, take some food every week to the gates of the camp in which her father was imprisoned:

... He thought that our efforts were absolutely lunatic. Once we held a family council to see whether there existed any possibilities of giving some assistance to my father, and if so what they were; but he only said: 'Set your heart at rest: you'll never see him again.'

Instead, at the end of the war, her father returned but he looked like a ghost (he died not many years later). Hety, who was very close to him, felt duty bound to continue his activity in the reborn Social Democratic Party; her husband did not agree, there was a quarrel, and he asked for and obtained a divorce. His second wife was a refugee from Eastern Prussia who, because of the two children, kept up a discreet relationship with Hety. Once, with regard to her father, Dachau and the Lagers, she said to her:

> Do not take it in bad part if I cannot bear to read or listen to these concerns of yours. When we had to escape it was terrible; and the worst thing was that we were forced to go down the route by which the Auschwitz prisoners had been evacuated. The road ran between two hedges of dead bodies. I would like to forget those images and I cannot: I continue to see them in my dreams.

Her father had just returned when Thomas Mann spoke on radio about Auschwitz, the gas and the crematoria.

> We all listened, deeply perturbed, and were silent for a long time. Papa paced back and forth, taciturn, brooding, until I asked him: 'But does it seem possible to you that people can be poisoned with gas, burnt, their hair, their skin, their teeth utilised?' And he, even though he did come from Dachau, answered: 'No, it is not thinkable. A Thomas Mann should not give credence to such horrors.' And yet it was all true: a few weeks later we had proof of it and were convinced.

In another letter of hers she had described their life in 'internal emigration':

> My mother had a very dear Jewish friend. She was a widow and lived alone, her children had emigrated, but she could not resolve to leave Germany. We too were persecuted, but we were 'politicals': it was different for us, and despite the many dangers we were fortunate. I will never forget the evening on which that woman came to us, in the dark, to tell us: 'Please, don't come to see me any longer, and excuse me if I do not come to see you. You understand, I would endanger you' . . . Naturally, we

continued to visit her until she was deported to Theresien-stadt. We never saw her again and we 'did' nothing for her: what could we have done? And yet the thought that nothing could be done still torments us: I beg you, try to understand.

She told me that in 1967 she had attended the Euthanasia Trial. One of the defendants, a physician, had declared in court that he had been personally ordered to give poison injections to the mental patients, and that he had refused because of his professional conscience; by contrast, operating the gas spigot had seemed disagreeable to him, but in fact tolerable. On returning home, Hety found her cleaning woman, a war widow, intent on her work, and her son cooking. They all three sat down at the table and she told the son what she saw and heard at the trial. And suddenly

... the woman put down her fork and interrupted aggressively: 'What is the point of all these trials they're having now? What could they do about it, our poor soldiers, if they gave them those orders? When my husband came on furlough from Poland, he told me: "Almost all we did was shoot Jews, shoot Jews all the time. My arm hurt from so much shooting." But what was he supposed to do, if they had given him those orders?' ... I discharged her, stifling the temptation to congratulate her on her poor husband fallen in the war ... So there, you see, here in Germany even today we live in the midst of this sort of people.

Hety worked many years for the Ministry of Culture of the Land Hessen: she was a diligent but impulsive functionary, the author of polemical reviews, the 'impassioned' organiser of conventions and meetings with young people, and just as impassioned about her Party's victories and defeats. After her retirement, which took place in 1978, her cultural life became richer: she wrote to me about travels, lectures, linguistic debates.

But above all, and throughout her life, she was avid, even famished for human encounters: the one with me, durable and fertile, was only one of many. 'My destiny drives me towards men with a destiny,' she wrote to me once: but more than a destiny what drove her was a vocation. She searched for such persons, found them, put them in touch with one another, extremely curious about their encounters or collisions. It is she who gave me the address of Jean Améry and mine to him, but on one condition: that we both would send her carbon copies of the letters we would exchange. We did. She also played an important role in helping me track down that Dr Müller, the chemist in Auschwitz, later my supplier of chemical products and the penitent about whom I spoke in the Vanadium chapter in *The Periodic Table*. He had been a colleague of her ex-husband's. She had also asked for copies of the Müller dossier, to which she had a right; and she wrote intelligent letters to him about me and to me about him, with dutiful cross-mailings of all copies – 'for your information'.

Only on one occasion did we (or at least did I) perceive a divergence. In 1966 Albert Speer was released from the Inter-Allied Spandau gaol. As is known, he had been Hitler's court architect, but in 1943 he was appointed Minister of the War Industry; in that position he was to a great extent responsible for the organisation of the factories in which *we* died of over-work and hunger. At Nuremberg he had been the only one among the defendants to plead guilty, also for things he had not known about; indeed, precisely for not having wanted to know about them. He was sentenced to twenty years of con-finement, which he employed in writing his prison memoirs, published in Germany in 1975. Hety at first hesitated, then she read them, and was profoundly perturbed by them. She asked Speer for a meeting, which lasted two hours. She left him Langbein's book on Auschwitz and a copy of *If This Is A Man*, telling him that it was his duty to read them. He gave her a copy of his Spandau diaries for Hety to send on to me.

I received and read these diaries, which bear the mark of a

cultivated and lucid mind and a change of heart that seems sincere (but an intelligent man knows how to simulate). In them Speer comes through as a Shakespearean character of boundless ambition, so great as to blind and contaminate him, but not a barbarian, coward or serf. I would gladly have eschewed this reading, because for me judging is painful; particularly as regards Speer, not a simple man, and a culprit who has paid. I wrote to Hety with a trace of irritation: 'What impelled you to visit Speer? Curiosity? A sense of duty? A "mission"?'

She answered:

I hope you understood the correct meaning of the gift of that book. Your question is also correct. I wanted to look into his face: look at how a man is made who allowed himself to be the succubus of Hitler, and became his creature. He says, and I believe him, that for him the Auschwitz slaughter is a trauma. He's obsessed by the question of how he could 'not want to see or know', in short, block everything out. I do not think he's trying to find justification; he would like to understand what, for him too, it is impossible to understand. He appears to me as a man who does not falsify, fights loyally, and torments himself over his past. For me, he has become 'a key': he is a symbolic personage, the symbol of German aberration. He read Langbein's book with great pain, and he promised me that he would also read yours. I will keep you informed of his reactions.

These reactions, to my relief, never arrived: if I had been forced (as is the custom among civilised persons) to answer a letter from Albert Speer, I would have had some problems. In 1978, apologising to me because of the disapproval she had scented in my letters, Hety visited Speer a second time and came back disappointed. She found him senile, egocentric, pompous and stupidly proud of his past as a Pharaonic architect. Thereafter the substance of our letters moved towards subjects which were more alarming because more current: the Moro affair, the escape of Kappler, the sudden death of the Baader-Meinhoff terrorist gang in the Stammheim super-gaol. She was inclined to believe the official thesis of suicide; I was doubtful. Speer died in 1981, and Hety, unexpectedly, in 1983.

Our friendship, almost exclusively epistolary, was long and fruitful, often cheerful; strange, if I think of the enormous difference between our human itineraries and the geographic and linguistic distance between us, less strange if I recognise that among all my German readers she was the only one 'with clean credentials' and therefore not entangled in guilt feelings; and that her curiosity was and is mine, and this led her to rack her brains over the same themes I have discussed in this book.

# Conclusion

The experiences that we survivors of the Nazi Lagers carry within us are extraneous to the new Western generation, and become ever more extraneous as the years pass. For the young people of the 1950s and 1960s these were events connected with their fathers: they were spoken about in the family, memories of them still preserved the freshness of things seen. For the young people of the 1980s, they are matters associated with their grandfathers: distant, blurred, 'historical'. These young people are besieged by today's problems, different, urgent: the nuclear threat, unemployment, the depletion of resources, the demographic explosion, technologies which are frenetically innovative and to which they must adjust. The world's configuration is profoundly changed. Europe is no longer the centre of the planet. The colonial empires have yielded to the pressure of the peoples of Asia and Africa, thirsting for independence, and were dissolved not without tragedies and struggles between the new nations. Germany, split in two for an indefinite future, has become 'respectable', and in fact holds the destiny of Europe in its hands. The United States–Soviet Union diarchy, born from the Second World War, persists; but the ideologies on which the governments of the two sole victors of the last conflict are based have lost much of their credibility and splendour. A sceptical generation stands at the threshold of adulthood, bereft not of ideals but of certainties, indeed distrustful of the grand revealed truth: disposed instead to accept the small truths, changeable from month to month on the convulsed wave of cultural fashions, whether guided or wild.

For us to speak with the young becomes ever more difficult. We see it as a duty, and at the same time as a risk: the risk of appearing anachronistic, of not being listened to. We must be listened to: above and beyond our personal experiences, we have collectively been the witnesses of a fundamental, unexpected event, fundamental precisely because unexpected, not foreseen by anyone. It took place in the teeth of all forecasts; it happened in Europe. Incredibly, it happened that an entire civilised people, just issued from the fervid cultural flowering of Weimar, followed a buffoon whose figure today inspires laughter, and yet Adolf Hitler was obeyed and his praises were sung right up to the catastrophe. It happened, therefore it can happen again: this is the core of what we have to say.

It can happen, and it can happen everywhere. I do not intend to nor can I say that it will happen; as I pointed out earlier, it is not very probable that all the factors that unleashed the Nazi madness will again occur simultaneously but precursory signs loom before us. Violence, 'useful' or 'useless', is there before our eyes: it snakes either through sporadic and private episodes, or government lawlessness, both in what we call the first and the second worlds, that is to say, the parliamentary democracies and countries in the Communist area. In the third world it is endemic or epidemic. It only awaits its new buffoon (there is no dearth of candidates) to organise it, legalise it, declare it necessary and mandatory and so contaminate the world. Few countries can be considered immune to a future tide of violence generated by intolerance, lust for power, economic difficulties, religious or political fanaticism, and racialist attritions. It is therefore necessary to sharpen our senses, distrust the prophets, the enchanters, those who speak and write 'beautiful words' unsupported by intelligent reasons.

It has obscenely been said that there is a need for conflict: that mankind cannot do without it. It has also been said that local conflicts, violences in the streets, factories and stadiums, are equivalent of generalised war and preserve us from it, as *le petit mal*, the epileptic equivalent, preserves from *le grand mal*. It has been observed that never before in Europe did forty years go by without a war: such a long European peace is supposedly an historical anomaly.

These are captious and suspect arguments. Satan is not necessary: there is no need for wars and violences, under any circumstances. There do not exist problems that cannot be solved around a table, provided there is good will and reciprocal trust: or even reciprocal fear, as the present interminable stalled situation seems to demonstrate, a situation in which the greatest powers confront each other with cordial or threatening faces, but have no restraint when it comes to unleashing (or allow the unleashing) of bloody wars among those 'protected' by them, supplying sophisticated weapons, spies, mercenaries and military advisers instead of arbiters of peace.

Nor is the theory of preventive violence acceptable: from violence only violence is born, following a pendular action that becomes more frenzied as time goes by rather than dying down. In actuality, many signs lead us to think of a genealogy of today's violence that branches out precisely from the violence that was dominant in Hitler's Germany. Certainly it was not absent before, in the remote and recent past: nevertheless, even in the midst of the insensate slaughter of the First World War there survived the traits of a reciprocal respect between the antagonists, a vestige of humanity toward prisoners and unarmed citizens, a tendential respect for treaties, a believer might say 'a certain fear of God'. The adversary was neither a demon nor a worm. After the Nazi *Gott mit uns*, everything changed. Goering's terrorist bombings were answered by the 'carpet' bombings of the Allies. The destruction of a people and a civilisation was proved to be possible, and desirable both in itself and as an instrument of rule. The massive exploitation of slave labour was learned by Hitler in the school of Stalin, but in the Soviet Union it was brought back again, multiplied at the end of the war. The exodus of brains from Germany and Italy, together with the fear of being surpassed by Nazi scientists, gave birth to the nuclear bombs. Desperate, the Jewish survivors, in flight from Europe after the great shipwreck, have created in the bosom of the Arab world an island of Western civilisation, a portentous palingenesis of Judaism, and the pretext for renewed hatred. After the defeat, the silent Nazi diaspora has taught the art of persecution and torture to the military and the political men of a dozen countries, on the shores of the Mediterranean, the Atlantic and Pacific. Many new tyrants have kept in their drawer Adolf Hitler's *Mein Kampf*: with a few changes perhaps, and the substitution of a few names, it can still come in handy.

The Hitlerian example demonstrated to what an extent a war fought in the industrial era can be devastating even without having recourse to nuclear weapons. During the last twenty years, the ill-fated Vietnamese enterprise, the Falklands conflict, the Iran–Iraq war, and the events in Cambodia and Afghanistan confirm it. Yet, it has also demonstrated (not in the rigorous sense of mathematicians, unfortunately) that, at least sometimes, at least in part, historical crimes are punished. The powerful of the Third Reich ended on the gallows or in suicide; the German people suffered a Biblical 'massacre' of the first born that decimated a generation, and a partition of their country that put an end to century-old German pride. It is not absurd to assume that if Nazism had not shown itself so very ruthless from the start, the alliance among its adversaries would not have been formed, or would have broken up before the end of the conflict, shattered. The world war willed by the Nazis and the Japanese was a suicidal war: all wars should be feared as such.

To the stereotypes I reviewed in the seventh chapter I would finally like to add one more. More often and more insistently as that time recedes, we are asked by the young who our 'torturers' were, of what cloth were they made. The term torturers alludes to our ex-guardians, the SS, and is in my opinion inappropriate: it brings to mind twisted individuals, ill-born, sadists, afflicted by an original flaw. Instead, they were made of our same cloth, they were average human beings, averagely intelligent, averagely wicked: save for exceptions, they were not monsters, they had our faces, but they had been

reared badly. They were, for the greater part, diligent followers and functionaries: some fanatically convinced of the
Nazi doctrine, many indifferent, or fearful of punishment, or
desirous of a good career, or too obedient. All of them had
been subjected to the terrifying miseducation provided for and
imposed by the schools created in accordance with the wishes
of Hitler and his collaborators, and then completed by the SS
drill. Many had joined this militia because of the prestige it
conferred, because of its omnipotence, or even just to escape
family problems. Some, very few in truth, had changes of heart,
requested transfers to the front lines, gave cautious help to
prisoners or chose suicide. Let it be clear that to a greater or
lesser degree all were responsible, but it must be just as clear
that behind their responsibility stands that great majority of
Germans, who accepted in the beginning, out of mental laziness, myopic calculation, stupidity, and national pride, the
'beautiful words' of Corporal Hitler, followed him as long as
luck and the lack of scruples favoured him, were swept away
by his ruin, afflicted by deaths, misery and remorse, and re-
habilitated a few years later as the result of an unprincipled
political game.